COLLINSFORT VILLAGE

joe ekaitis

COLLINSFORT VILLAGE

JOE EKAITIS

WindRiver Publishing
Silverton, Idaho

Queries, comments or correspondence concerning this work should be directed to the author and submitted to WindRiver Publishing at:

Authors@WindRiverPublishing.com

Information regarding this work or other works published by WindRiver Publishing, Inc., and instructions for submitting manuscripts for review for publication, can be found at:

www.WindRiverPublishing.com

Collinsfort Village
Copyright ©2005 by Joe Ekaitis
Cover Design and Illustrations by Nick Greenwood

Library of Congress Control Number: 2005925290
ISBN-13 978-1-886249-21-9
ISBN-10 1-886249-21-0

First Printing 2005

Printed in the U.S.A. by Malloy, Inc., on acid-free paper

To my wife Cathy, Jim Lane,
Tassie, Wanda, Karsten,
and to anyone who ever wanted to
walk down the street with a griffin.

Griff 'n' Bear It

CHAPTER 1

The Fourth Saturday of Every Other Month

"Well, would you look at *this*!" exclaimed Bear as he banged around in the kitchen of the cave. "Just enough coffee for that first pot in the morning!" He tramped from the cabinet to the calendar and rustled its pages. "Wow, and on grocery day! What a lucky coincidence, eh, Griff?" Griff pretended not to hear Bear shouting. He buried himself even deeper beneath his pile of straw.

Bear took a box of cold cereal from the cabinet and picked up an empty glass bowl. He stood in the tall archway of Griff's bedroom and held the box high above the bowl as he poured.

Ping! Ping! Ping-a-dee-ping-ping! Ping! Ping! Ping!

When the pinging stopped, the box was empty, but the bowl was only half full. Bear shook the box a few times and peeked inside it.

"Aw, fudge! We're out of Cocoa Grenades, too! Good thing it's grocery day!"

A massive head emerged from the straw. It resembled a gigantic golden eagle with the ears of a huge jackal. Two big steely eyes glared down at Bear with pure malice.

Bear tucked the empty cereal box under his arm. He reached into his blue jeans' pocket, pulled out a folded piece of paper and held it up. He didn't even flinch as a sharp-taloned claw swept toward him and snatched the paper from his paw.

The giant half-eagle, half-lion creature sat up. Bits of straw tumbled off his head as he unfolded the paper and scrutinized it. "Are you sure we need all this?" he grumbled.

"You said we were having roast beef and Yorkshire pudding for dinner tomorrow," said Bear, returning to the kitchen.

Griff rose up on his back legs to his full standing height of about twenty feet. He shook the remaining straw out of his fur and feathers before ambling to the kitchen where Bear poured him an enormous mug of coffee. Griff sat on the floor at the kitchen table while Bear settled into a chair.

Bear had already separated the newspaper into the sections each of them usually read. He took the Sports, Comics and Auto pages while Griff, with a tiny pair of wire-rimmed reading glasses perched on his beak, pored over the Arts, Books and Fine Food sections. With the precision of a surgeon, Griff used a single razor-sharp talon to cut out a few coupons. He peered over his reading glasses at Bear, who was immersed in an article about the restoration of a 1959 Cadillac Biarritz.

"I'll give you fifty dollars if you'll…"

"Don't even start," said Bear without looking up, halting the same conversation that never quite got underway on the fourth Saturday of every alternate month.

Griff and Bear were two unusual creatures. Under the pen name Karolyne von Frankenburgh—a recluse who refused to be photographed—Griff was the successful author of a series of myth and legend novels, though he had never really cared for the trappings of wealth. He anonymously donated much of his income from writing to charity. He had little need for most creature comforts. Being a griffin, he preferred burying himself in a pile of straw when he slept, and he sat directly on the floor of the cave when he ate his meals, watched TV, read or wrote.

Bear was also unique. At seven feet from his ears to the ground, he was every inch a brown bear—despite wearing human-style clothes and holding a respectable job. He slept in a king-size bed and drove a restored 1968 Chevy Suburban that his friends described as "Cherry Supreme."

Bear had a cousin who worked for the Forest Service, preaching a gospel of wildfire prevention. His well-known relation lived in a sparsely furnished log cabin, but Bear outfitted his cave with all the comforts of modern living, including satellite TV and high-speed Internet.

As a natural-born climber who was also adept at navigating subterranean passages, Bear worked for the local telephone company repairing both overhead and underground cables. He was welcome in town to do his work, the grocery shopping, or even to take in a movie, but he could not afford the high cost of having a house specially built for his size.

So, he and Griff shared a cave high in the foothills of the Rocky Mountains overlooking the suburb of Collinsfort Village.

They also shared the task of shopping for groceries every month. Since he was about the same height as a basketball player and as nimble on his feet, Bear was welcomed by the people at the supermarket. In fact, he was something of a celebrity. On his last trip to town, he had been greeted by a tabloid TV crew who wanted to film a feature story about him.

But when Griff's turn came to do the shopping, things were very different. Griff dreaded the outing as much as the supermarket staff dreaded his arrival. Yet, Griff was honor bound to do his share of the chores. He was also a slave to his fastidious tastes. He trusted only himself or Bear to pick out the ingredients for his culinary masterpieces, so he grudgingly took his turn at the shopping.

Anywhere else in town, Griff was warmly welcomed. With his fifty-foot wingspan he was majestic in flight, dwarfing the bald eagles that often fell into formation behind him. On the ground he walked with the dignity and elegance of a true gentleman. He greeted everyone he met with courtesy. When he shook a man's hand or kissed the hand of a woman, he would bow so low that the person did not have to raise his or her elbow above shoulder height.

Strolling past the Village Book Nook always amused him. No one in town had ever suspected that he was really the author of the "Sci-Fi/Fantasy Pick of the Month" featured in the store's window. To millions of readers around the world Griff was Fräulein Karolyne von Frankenburgh, the reclusive Austrian expatriate who spun tales of fantasy and magic from the isolation of an abandoned farm in a remote region of post-Communist Bulgaria. To the folks of Collinsfort Village, he was just Griff, the gentlemanly giant who read stories to children at the library three Saturdays a month.

But when he arrived at the supermarket, all that changed. Griff was forced to drop down on his claws and wait for the sliding automatic doors to open all the way before he crossed the threshold. Then he would reach inside with one arm, flatten his head and chest to the floor, angle his shoulders, and drag himself halfway through the door. Rising up on his claws, he would then shimmy his legs through and swing his tail in before the doors started to close.

Since an eagle's claws are meant for grasping and perching, and a lion's feet are meant for walking, Griff usually walked upright. But the supermarket's low ceiling forced him to do his shopping on all fours. Meanwhile, the tips of his wings were constantly knocking items from the shelves that lined the narrow aisles. The store manager would not let Griff have a shopping cart unless he took along the cleanup cart as well. By the time he found everything on his shopping list, Griff's back ached and his pride had been bruised from mopping up the broken bottles and packages left in his wake.

So, steeling himself against the humiliation, Griff now tucked the shopping list and his coupons into an oversized, zippered wallet, which dangled from a thin leather lanyard. He slipped the lanyard over his head, swung the wallet around so it settled between his wings and cinched the lanyard up around his neck to keep it from falling off in flight. After finishing his breakfast of a dozen eggs, a pound of bacon and eight slices of toast with imported black raspberry preserves, he got up from the table and deposited his dishes in the kitchen sink. On his way out, he paused and turned back.

"Bear, can you take a look at my paper shredder? It jammed yesterday."

"Right after I wax the Suburban," responded Bear, again without looking up from the Sports page.

Griff stepped outside the cave and padded to the edge of the sheer cliff that overlooked the town. He took a single step over the precipice, free falling a few hundred feet before extending his wings and gliding to the ground. He landed near the city limits, right next to the Shakespeare Riding Academy and Stables.

The horses were so used to seeing Griff that his approach did not spook them at all. Most of them ignored him, but a strapping chestnut stallion trotted to the fence, hoping for a treat.

"Sorry, Romeo, but I haven't been to the market yet," said Griff. "Oh, and Dennis, you're only wasting your time. Griffins do *not* eat horses, no matter what Karolyne von Frankenburgh might write."

Dennis Pearson, a local eight-year-old, slipped out of his hiding place behind a tractor. From the time he could walk, Dennis had taken a keen interest in Griff, and once he was old enough to read, he could not read enough about griffins. On his T-shirt was the word "Frankenburgh" in an old European script and a victim's-eye view of a large fierce-looking griffin swooping in for the kill. He carried a book by Karolyne von Frankenburgh under his arm.

"I know how you did that!" he called as he ran after Griff.

Griff slowed down so Dennis could keep up.

"Did what?"

"You couldn't see me, but you knew where I was. Karolyne von Frankenburgh says that what a griffin can't see, he can always smell or hear. That's how the blind griffin in *Trio of Terror* hunted down the ogre and squished him until his guts splattered like a rotten tomato.... Do ogres really smell that bad?"

"How would I know? That's a character in a book. I've never met Fräulein von Frankenburgh, and I doubt she has ever met a real griffin."

Dennis ran around in front of Griff and stopped. He opened the book to a half-page illustration, took out a folded piece of paper and held it up to Griff. "Can a real griffin do this?"

Griff unfolded the paper, looked at it, and immediately averted his eyes.

"Please, Dennis, breakfast hasn't gone down yet!" He held the paper at arm's length as if it were a rotting piece of meat.

"See? I copied it from *Monarch of the Mages*!" Dennis held up the open book for comparison.

Griff took a quick glance at the book's simple black and white drawing of a griffin hoisting a slain dragon into the air. He judged it against Dennis' larger full-color interpretation. Line for line, Dennis had accurately reproduced the illustration, but with a few over-the-top embellishments.

"Dennis, you did a lot more than just copy it," said Griff. He squatted down and held the picture at Dennis' eye level.

Dennis closed the book and tucked it under his arm. "What do you mean?"

"Well, for one thing, the griffin in your picture looks exactly like me, and instead of a castle, you've drawn the riding academy in the background. Secondly, if I really could rip out a dragon's heart, there'd be nothing to pump the blood, thus it wouldn't have gushed all over my feathers like this. With my feathers matted down, I'd never get off the ground, much less carry a dead dragon twice my size. And why is there a horse dangling by its tail from my beak?"

Dennis' face drooped. "Are you saying it's not a good picture?"

"Quite the opposite, Dennis, it's very good. So good, in fact, that if I keep looking at it, you're going to be wearing my breakfast." He shuddered as he handed the drawing back.

Dennis brightened up. "You mean griffins can throw up? Cool!"

Griff sighed. He gently rested a claw on Dennis' shoulder and spoke in a fatherly tone.

"Dennis, don't you ever read books like *The Wind in the Willows* or *Little House on the Prairie*?"

"Nope."

"Maybe you should. Eight years old is a little young for Karolyne von Frankenburgh."

9

Dennis' blue eyes narrowed into a defiant glare. "I'm almost nine, Griff. Eight years and seven months is almost nine. Besides, it's not my fault. Kevin leaves them out, so I read them."

"Tell your brother if he doesn't start putting his books on a higher shelf, he'll find out the hard way what a real griffin can do to a teenage boy."

Dennis' eyes widened once more. "What are you going to do to him? Can I watch?"

Griff stood up. "Good day, Master Pearson." Without another word, he set off for the market at his normal walking pace, quickly leaving Dennis behind.

As Dennis turned to go home, a piece of paper flitted past his face and landed at his feet. The paper was a partly shredded royalty statement from Chrestus & Minos. Dennis recognized the name as the publisher of Karolyne von Frankenburgh's novels. Most of the addressee's name was missing, leaving only a list of titles and the author's earnings.

```
FRANKENBURGH: MONARCH       $2,314.37
FRANKENBURGH: PRINCE        $1,368.32
FRANKENBURGH: WIZARD'S        $624.42
FRANKENBURGH: FESTIVAL      $3,455.12
FRANKENBURGH: CELESTIAL     $4,211.19
FRANKENBURGH: TRIO          $3,747.91
```

Dennis correctly deduced the full titles of *Monarch of the Mages*, *Prince of the Sky*, *The Wizard's Conundrum*, *Festival of Sorcerers*, *Celestial Cotillion* and *Trio of Terror* from the one-word abbreviations. He folded the paper along its creases. The address lined up as it would appear in a windowed envelope. Only the last two letters of the addressee's name were still legible, "–in," but the address was clear:

P.O. Box 862
Collinsfort Village, CO   80524

"Whoa!" exclaimed Dennis. "She lives HERE! Right here in Collinsfort Village!"

Dennis wanted to tell someone—*anyone*—what he had just discovered, but by now Griff was so far away that Dennis would never be able to catch up with him.

Hmm… maybe I better wait until I have more proof, thought Dennis, *she could be anybody. If I'm wrong, I could get into a lot of trouble.*

He slipped the royalty statement into his book and headed home while formulating a plan to find out who in town might be Karolyne von Frankenburgh.

Meanwhile, Griff had just arrived at the supermarket to find the manager already waiting with the cleanup cart.

"Morning, Griff," he said as Griff squeezed his way through the automatic door marked ENTER. The manager nudged the cart toward him.

Griff draped a claw over the cart's handle. "Morning, Earl," he mumbled.

Back at the cave, Bear put the breakfast dishes in the dishwasher. He took a can of expensive carnauba car wax from a cabinet of cleaning supplies and walked out to his Suburban with three pairs of freshly laundered cotton gym socks and a stack of new cloth diapers that had already been washed once. He pulled one of the socks over his right paw and used it to apply a six-inch by six-inch square of wax to the vehicle's paint.

Then, holding one of the diapers in his other paw, he carefully studied the patch of wax, waiting for the exact moment when it was dry enough to buff off.

Griff had once observed the way Bear waxed the Suburban and could not resist looking up the word "obsessive" in the dictionary. To his surprise, he did not find a picture of Bear next to the entry.

For Bear, waxing his SUV was like meditation—it caused him to lose all track of time.

Nearly four hours later, with one fender still to go, Bear heard heavy footsteps approaching. It was Griff, carrying a month's worth of groceries in plastic shopping bags that dangled from his talons. Hunched over in pain, he plodded along the dirt road toward the cave instead of flying up the side of the mountain. His right wing was crumpled oddly.

"What happened to you?" asked Bear.

"They installed a new automatic exit door at the supermarket, and I couldn't get through before it closed," Griff said wearily.

Bear examined Griff's mangled wing. "That looks pretty nasty. Is it broken?"

"No, but I lost enough flight feathers to ground me for a few weeks. It'll stick out like that until they grow back."

He went inside and put away the groceries. Since it was his turn to make dinner he set out the ingredients for a pot of chili and a pan of cornbread. The chili recipe called for coarsely chopped onions, but Griff was in such a dark mood that he ended up pulverizing them. He beat the corn bread batter so fiercely that it came out of the oven as light and airy as a cornmeal angel food cake.

After dinner, Griff's disposition still hadn't improved, and it showed in his writing that evening. He sat down at his writing table and switched on both the lamp and his refurbished IBM Selectric typewriter. Picking up an unsharpened pencil in each claw, he used the eraser ends to strike the keys. In about an hour he had dashed out another chapter in Fräulein Karolyne von Frankenburgh's latest epic.

The chapter described a gory battle between the hero (a griffin, of course) and an evil sea serpent. It ended with a pirate ship sinking under a barrage of sea serpent body parts.

Griff always left his writing out where Bear could look it over, but after reading this latest chapter, Bear had to step outside the cave and take several deep breaths of fresh air to ward off an attack of nausea.

"Is it too long?" asked Griff as Bear handed back the graphic twelve-page moment-to-moment battle account.

Bear swallowed a dose of pink stomach medicine. "No. It's just… too *much.*"

Before going to bed, Griff reread the chapter and realized what Bear had meant. He woke up in a cold sweat a few hours later after dreaming he was the sea serpent from his own story. He stayed up until dawn, rewriting the entire chapter.

CHAPTER 2

Shadowing the Bruin

Griff stood outside the cave, facing into the wind. A month had passed and the flight feathers on his right wing had grown back, but he still needed to test his flying ability. He extended his wings stiffly and began flapping, first slowly, then faster, causing a downward rush of air similar to a helicopter's prop wash.

Griff shut his eyes and rolled his claws into fists. He screeched in agony as he rose into the air. At a height of about three feet he stopped and returned to the ground with a slight thud, gasping for breath.

Just then, Bear walked out of the cave. He was wearing his cross-trainers, a pair of gym trunks and a T-shirt. A runner's wallet hung from a lanyard around his neck, and in his paw were his keys and the month's shopping list.

"Invented the airplane yet, Orville Wright?" he quipped as he walked to his SUV.

"Very funny, Wilbur," said Griff, still panting and resting his claws on his knees.

Bear climbed into the Suburban and started the engine. After buckling his seat belt, he shifted the vehicle's Hydra-Matic into drive and waved the grocery list out the window as he drove past his cavemate. "You've got one more month to get your wings back!"

Griff watched until the Suburban disappeared around the first bend in the road. With Bear out of sight, he stopped panting, straightened up and spread his wings. In five powerful wing beats, he was airborne. He climbed high enough to keep the Suburban in view, while making sure that his shadow fell directly on the vehicle so Bear could not see him.

Griff wanted to know why Bear always went shopping in a good mood and came home just as happy, while Griff usually came home feeling as if he didn't have a friend left in the whole world. The people in town liked Griff, but they *loved* Bear, and Griff could not help but wonder why.

While Bear stopped at the post office, Griff circled slowly overhead, high enough that anyone on the ground would think he was just another bird in the sky.

Inside the post office, Dennis stood on a step stool at the copy machine and pretended he was copying a page from a book. He kept an eye on box 862. When anyone came into the building, Dennis would drop a quarter into the copier and make a big show of positioning the book. As soon as the customer left, he would press the coin return button and get ready to repeat the performance. Dennis had been staking out the postbox lobby since the day he found the royalty statement. It had been a month, and no one had checked box 862.

Bear opened the door and held it for a woman pushing a baby stroller. He glanced at Dennis. "Hey, Dennis," he said as he passed the copier.

Dennis went into his act. "Whassup, Bear?" He dropped the quarter into the coin slot while watching Bear from the corner of his eye.

Bear took the mail out of box 327 and then crossed the

lobby to the 800s. He inserted a tiny key into box 862, opened it and removed its contents.

Dennis gasped out loud.

Surprised by the sound, Bear turned around. He was greeted by a pair of bulging eyes and a gaping mouth etched into a ghostly white face.

"Are you *okay*, Dennis?" he asked.

Dennis' mouth quivered, but no sound came out.

"Dennis, it's just me, Bear. You-Know-Whose cousin. I got you his autograph when he came to town for Fire Prevention Week, remember?"

Dennis leaped down from the step stool and nearly tore the post office door from its hinges as he made an abrupt getaway. A second later he darted back into the building, hit the coin return on the copier and snatched his book and quarter from the machine. With one more unbelieving look at Bear, he dashed out the door.

Not sure what to make of Dennis' behavior, Bear climbed back into the Suburban and drove off.

From the air, Griff followed Bear to the outdoor basketball courts at Collinsfort Village High School. He landed just out of sight behind the Coyotes' Den gymnasium, flattened himself to the ground and peeked around the corner of the building.

"So, who needs a break?" called Bear as he jumped from the driver's seat.

A player named Larry waved to Bear then took a seat on the sidelines, wiping the sweat from his face as he sat down. "If you're selling, I'm buying," he called.

Bear trotted onto the court and was soon scoring layups and slam dunks with an ease that contradicted the old saying "clumsy as a bear." Forty-five minutes later he announced, "That's all she wrote, gentlemen!" and strode back to the Suburban.

Griff made a mental note: *must read up on basketball.* He took to the air once more to see where Bear was headed next.

Bear drove a few blocks and turned down a residential street. He parked at the curb where several young girls were playing hopscotch.

Griff hid in the branches of a nearby tree.

"Hi, Bear!" yelled the hopscotch players as the big bear stepped from his SUV. A referee's whistle and a stopwatch dangled from his neck.

Bear played a few rounds of hopscotch and then announced, "Warm-up's over. Time to hop with the big kangaroos. Let's play a little Fancy-Foot." He slipped the whistle and the stop-watch from around his neck and handed them to one of the girls. "Call it, Julie."

"A baker's dozen, no stone, a foul restarts the count but not the clock, three fouls and you're out."

"And who am I up against?"

"Megan. She holds the record with forty-eight seconds and no fouls."

Bear turned to face Megan, who giggled and tried to hide behind her playmates. He brought an imaginary phone to his ear while keeping his eyes on her. "Hello, *Guinness Book of World Records*?" he said in a deep, rumbling growl. "This is Bear. Get ready to stop the presses." He hung up the invisible phone and faced the hopscotch court with his arms at his side.

Julie started a short countdown. "Three... two... one!" She blew the referee's whistle, and Bear leaped into action, ex-pertly planting the toes of his size 17 extra wide cross-trainers completely within each square. While Julie called out the time at five-second intervals the rest of the girls cheered and counted off Bear's trips up and down the hopscotch court.

At thirty seconds, Bear had completed eight circuits. He made the ninth trip backwards.

"Nothing in the rule book says I can't," he smirked. He closed his eyes on the tenth trip. "The hard way!" he bellowed.

"Forty-five!" shouted Julie as Bear completed his eleventh circuit. Even Megan was cheering him on.

"Twelve… thirteen!"

Bear jumped off the hopscotch court, feigned an attack of exhaustion and dropped to one knee. After a few noisy, wheezing breaths, he stood up as everyone turned their attention to Julie. She was peering intently at the stopwatch's dial.

"Forty-nine and three-fifths seconds!" she announced.

"Darn!" said Bear in mock disappointment. "Sunk by my own showboat! Guess I gotta go home and practice."

Julie handed him the whistle and stopwatch as he headed back to the Suburban.

"Bye-bye, Bear!" the girls called after him.

Bear pulled the SUV away from the curb and headed straight to the supermarket.

From his hidden perch, Griff blinked in amazement.

"That's it?" he said to himself. "Basketball and hopscotch?" He dropped from the tree to the ground and strolled past the hopscotch players on the opposite side of the street.

"Hi, Griff!" called one of the girls.

Griff pretended to be surprised.

"What are you going to read for us next Saturday?" she asked.

"I'm on my way to the library right now to pick it out!" said Griff, not admitting that he had already selected *The Griffin's*

Apprenticeship, a rare children's book by Fräulein Karolyne von Frankenburgh.

The Collinsfort Village Public Library, with its wide, fourteen-foot-tall double doors and twenty-four-foot-high ceiling, was one of the few indoor places where Griff felt comfortable. Nearly every weekday, he would spend the morning reading at the library. But first, he would stop by the espresso stand in the park for a forty-ounce, double strong latte, which he poured into his spill-proof mug. Then he would head straight to the library.

The regular patrons barely took notice when Griff pulled open both double doors, stooped low enough to pass under the doorway and strode into the central atrium where he could resume his full standing height. In fact, they considered him a handy addition to the library. Griff didn't need a ladder to take a book from most of the higher shelves. And anyone wanting a bookmark needed only to take one of Griff's cast-off feathers from the vases on the reading tables.

Out-of-town visitors were always impressed by the realistic life-size statue of a griffin seated on the atrium steps silently reading. They were then startled when the "statue" came to life and turned the page. One visitor was even heard to say, "Cool! It's animatronic!" To which Griff could not resist answering, "No, Roman Catholic."

Story time on the first three Saturdays of the month transformed the library into an almost magical place. Depending on the story he was reading and the mood he was in, Griff would either sit upright on the top step with his feet resting at the bottom of the atrium, or stretch out on the floor and prop himself up on his elbows. Either way, the children would surround him, a few snuggling against his warm coat, others taking positions up and down the steps.

Griff read with a voice that was both powerful and soothing as it floated gently into every corner of the library. It was never intrusive or distracting, an amazing feat for a creature whose loudest shriek could burst a dragon's eardrums and send cracks running through a castle wall.

As an extra treat, every year beginning on the evening of the winter solstice and continuing nightly through New Year's Day, Griff would entertain a packed library with his recitation of Charles Dickens' *A Christmas Carol.* He even acted out all of the parts himself, from Ebenezer Scrooge to Tiny Tim.

But this was the fourth Saturday of the month, and the winter solstice was still months away; Griff had work to do.

He sat down at one of the computers and perched his reading glasses on his beak as he scanned the electronic card catalog. With a pair of pencils from his wallet he typed two keywords into the SEARCH field: "basketball" and "hopscotch." A list of titles filled the screen. Griff jotted down a few and gave the list to a library assistant since some of the books were tucked away on the library's narrower aisles.

"This is pretty lightweight stuff compared to what you usually read, Griff," she said.

"Variety, Miranda," Griff responded. "You know… spice of life and all that. One is never too old to learn something new."

Miranda soon returned with a stack of books from Griff's list. At the checkout desk she scanned them, and Griff scooped them up. As he left, he nearly tripped over Dennis who was standing just outside the library doors.

Dennis spoke in an eerie monotone.

"I have to tell you something, Griff. I know the truth."

"About what?"

"About Karolyne von Frankenburgh."

Griff looked around to make sure no one else had heard Dennis. He gestured for Dennis to follow him, and they walked to the city limits where only the horses at the Shakespeare Riding Academy would hear their conversation.

Dennis sat on the top rail of the fence surrounding the training track.

Griff leaned against the fence and in a calm reassuring tone said, "Tell me everything you know."

"Karolyne von Frankenburgh lives in Collinsfort Village," declared Dennis.

"Does she?" said Griff, hoping his cool reply would hide his surprise.

"No," said Dennis. "*He* lives in Collinsfort Village. She's a *he*."

"*He?*" said Griff, mimicking Dennis' emphasis. "And where in town does *he* live?"

"In a cave on the mountain. He comes to town just about every day, and no one knows he's really Karolyne von Frankenburgh. But I know... I have evidence."

"What sort of evidence?" said Griff, struggling to remain calm.

Dennis pulled a small manila envelope from his pocket and removed the royalty statement. He handed it to Griff.

"Where did you find this?" said Griff in a tone that made a horse named King Lear whinny in fear and bolt for the safety of his paddock.

Dennis blinked, but he didn't cower. "It fell from the air. Honest."

Griff straightened to his full height, crossed his arms and fixed a hard piercing stare on Dennis. He hoped Dennis would believe the myth that a griffin's big eagle eyes could see into a person's soul.

"Once more, Dennis, where did you find this?" he said slowly and deliberately.

Dennis returned an equally hard stare as he matched Griff's stern delivery. "I already told you. It fell from the air."

Griff sighed in defeat. Clearly, Dennis was telling the truth.

"Well, that was my fault, Dennis. I should have made sure this was disposed of properly, but I was careless. So, now that you know the truth, go ahead and ask anything you want about Karolyne von Frankenburgh."

"Did you always know she was really Bear?"

The question caught Griff off guard, but he spotted an opportunity to keep his secret safe. "Of course! I've known it ever since…"

"Ever since when?"

"Ever since I've known Bear! By the way, how did you figure it out? You must have done some extraordinary detective work."

Dennis nodded vigorously.

"I staked out the post office for a whole month, and I saw Bear picking up the mail from box 862, just like on that royalty paper."

"Extraordinary, indeed," said Griff. "Sherlock Holmes would be green with envy."

Griff was beginning to feel a twinge of guilt. This was far too easy. He had to give Dennis at least one chance to hear the truth.

"Dennis, would you believe me if I told you *I'm* really Karolyne von Frankenburgh, and Bear picks up the mail for me?"

Dennis' answer came back with a bluntness that nearly knocked Griff over.

"Nope."

"But I'm a griffin, and the hero in nearly every one of her books is a griffin."

"So? You won't even eat a horse. If you wrote a story, the griffin would make cookies and the dragon would bake them with his breath."

"And you think Bear writes about griffins that eat horses?"

Dennis nodded again. "Yep. I was watching a show about bears on the Animal Channel, and I saw this grizzly bear stop a charging moose by smashing it on the head. Then he ate the moose. It was cool! You could see the moose's insides! I'll bet Bear could do the same thing, but he won't. At least not when anyone's looking."

"Why not?"

"He doesn't want to blow his cover. If everyone knew Bear could stop a moose in its tracks, they wouldn't go near him."

"Take another look at the royalty statement," said Griff handing the paper back to Dennis. "Now, what's my full name? You've known it as long as you've known me."

"Errington F. Griffin," Dennis stated.

"Exactly. Griffin ends with the letters 'in,' just like the name on the royalty statement," said Griff, pointing a large but precise talon at the torn upper line. "Case closed."

He reached for the statement.

"Or *Bruin*," said Dennis, reeling in his arm before Griff could seize the statement. He slipped it into the envelope and made it vanish into his pocket so fast that it almost resembled a magician's parlor trick. "Bruin ends with 'in,' too, and Bear once told me his real name is Ursaline B. Bruin. He said his mom was hoping for a daughter."

It was obvious that Dennis had made up his mind and nothing was going to change it.

"I give up, Dennis," said Griff. "You're just too smart for me. I'll bet you already know what Bear would do to anyone foolish enough to reveal his secret identity."

Dennis thought for a moment. "The same thing that grizzly on TV did to the moose?"

Griff shook his head. He leaned closer and lowered his voice. "Worse. Much, much worse."

Dennis' jaw dropped. He gulped. "Worse?" he squeaked.

This time Griff nodded grimly.

"A grizzly doesn't tear his dinner into pieces no bigger than your hand and fling them over an area the size of a football field. Beneath Bear's mild-mannered exterior lurks a raging beast that can only be tamed by turning all that fury into literature. Now you know why the publisher asked me to keep an eye on him. At the first hint of trouble…" Griff tipped back his head and swept a single talon past his throat, "…shhhp! No more Bear, and no more Karolyne von Frankenburgh. It's a frightening responsibility, but if I ever have to go through with it, the world will never forgive you or me."

"You *or* me?" said Dennis.

"We're in this together now, Dennis. The moment Karolyne von Frankenburgh is gone the press will hunt us down like common criminals and plaster our faces all over the TV and the newspapers. We'll be the enemies of every one of her fans. You're the only person on earth who can keep that from happening."

Dennis looked around as if Griff were addressing someone else, but even the horses had fled from the sound of doom in Griff's voice.

"Me? How?"

"Never—and I do mean *never*—mention the name Karolyne von Frankenburgh in Bear's presence. Bear values his privacy and doesn't want to see the town overrun with fans trying to get a glimpse of him or mobbing him for an autograph. That's why he writes under a pen name and why he guards his secret so jealously. He does it as much for the people of Collinsfort Village as for himself. If we let him down, we'll be letting everyone down."

"Should I just stay away from him altogether?"

"No, no, anything but that," said Griff with a note of impending disaster. "Bear's instincts are as sharp as mine. If one tiny detail is out of place, it will only set him off and he'll strike with the speed of a mountain lion. I may not get there in time to save you, but I promise I'll bring along a bucket to carry away whatever is left of you, right after I finish him off."

"But I don't want to be carried away in a bucket! What should I do?" Dennis pleaded.

"Act as if you've seen nothing, heard nothing, and know nothing. If Bear's walking toward you on the sidewalk, *do not* cross the street to avoid him, but once he's passed you, don't let him out of your sight either. If he says 'Hi,' say it right back and make sure he hears you. Oh, and Bear can smell his own scent on anything he's handled, including that royalty statement. If he thinks it's in your possession, he'll claw his way through a brick wall just to get it back. So, for the sake of your very life, you never saw it and this conversation never took place. Do you understand?"

Dennis nodded in wide-eyed awe.

"Good," said Griff calmly. "Now, what else would you like to know about Karolyne von Frankenburgh?"

"Karolyne von *Who*?" said Dennis. He plunged his hand into his pocket and yanked out the envelope as if it were burning a hole in his jeans. "Never heard of her!" he declared as he slapped the envelope into Griff's waiting claw. He jumped down from the fence and took off for home.

Griff waited until Dennis was out of sight. Then he held up the envelope with a grin. "Come to Papa," he said with satisfaction. He kissed the paper and slipped it between the pages of *A Complete History of Hopscotch and Other Playground Games.*

Later that evening while Griff was hammering away on his typewriter, Bear plopped onto the couch in the living room. He picked up the universal remote and switched on the TV to watch a late season NBA game—Lakers vs. the Knicks. He didn't notice that the VCR came on at the same time, or that it was tuned to the same channel. When the game was over, Bear turned everything off and went to bed.

Griff stayed up as he often did when he was working on a particularly exciting chapter.

He stopped typing for a moment. Though Bear's bedroom door was closed, Griff's sharp hearing detected his friend's rasping snore. He picked up one of the library books as he got up from his writing table, went into the kitchen and took a bottle of cold-brewed gourmet root beer from the refrigerator. Returning to the living room, he settled himself on the floor next to the couch, picked up the remote control and rewound the tape in the VCR. Cautiously, he turned on the TV and lowered the volume. As the recorded basketball game got underway, Griff opened the library's copy of *NBA Basketball for Dummies* to page one.

CHAPTER 3

It's Showtime!

Bear smelled coffee. He was still in bed, but he could definitely smell coffee dribbling into the carafe of the twelve-cup German drip coffeemaker in the kitchen. He rolled over and checked the time on his clock radio: 6:57 a.m. Bear climbed out of bed, pulled on his robe and walked to the bedroom door. He remembered that not only was it Saturday, it was also the last Saturday of the month and Griff's turn to go to the supermarket.

Bear shuffled to the kitchen. He found Griff mixing pancake batter with a flourish while humming a medley of *Sweet Georgia Brown* and the jingle from ESPN's basketball telecasts.

Griff looked over his shoulder as Bear sat down.

"Great day to be alive, eh, Bear?"

Not yet fortified by his first cup of coffee, Bear could only mumble, "Pancakes?" as Griff poured him a mug of coffee.

"Not just *any* pancakes!" said Griff, putting down the carafe. He picked up the mixing bowl and scattered a generous claw full of blueberries over the top of the batter. "Wild blueberry pancakes! Picked 'em myself! Your own mother doesn't feed you like this!"

Griff folded the berries into the batter.

Bear sipped enough coffee to regain his ability to speak.

"My mother is the activities director at a home for retired circus animals in Sarasota. She's too busy and too far away to fix my breakfast."

Griff poured the batter onto the griddle, forming eight perfect pancakes.

"Remember," Bear cautioned. "Turn them over before…"

"…before the bubbles pop. It makes them lighter," Griff said, finishing the sentence. "I've been making pancakes since before your grandfather was a wee cub," he added with mock indignation. He flipped the pancakes over and allowed the second side to cook until they reached the perfect shade of brown. Then he deftly stacked them on a plate and placed them in front of Bear while taking a deep bow.

"Thank you, Jeeves," said Bear as he rose from his seat. He was about to get the pancake syrup from the cabinet when Griff slammed his foot down in Bear's path.

"Don't you *dare!*" he said sternly while bringing what looked like a bottle of brandy into view. With all the ceremony of a wine steward at a ritzy restaurant, Griff uncorked the bottle and wafted it first under his own beaked nostrils and then under Bear's shiny black nose. "Ah, the finest Vermont has to offer!" he said in a dreamy tone. He handed Bear the bottle of 100% pure maple syrup.

Dazed, Bear returned to his seat at the table and began spreading his pancakes with the contents of the butter dish.

"Are you feeling okay, Griff?"

"Couldn't be better! By the way, that's *real* butter, not margarine."

Bear picked up a few strips of bacon and examined them closely. "Did you butcher the pig and cure the bacon yourself?"

"Of course not!" said Griff. "But I *did* buy it directly from the smokehouse. I flew all night to make sure I was there when they opened."

"Griff, you're scaring me."

Griff splayed his claw across his chest and cocked his head. *"Moi?* I can't even scare a four-year-old when I'm reading the part where the Big Bad Wolf huffs and puffs and blows down the house of sticks." He sat down at the breakfast table with a triple batch of pancakes on his platter.

Bear looked over at the calendar.

"Do you know what day this is?"

"Of course I do," said Griff, digging into his pancakes. "It's the last Saturday of the month."

"It's your turn to do the grocery shopping."

"Yes, I know. Have you finished the shopping list yet?"

Bear had never seen Griff so eager to go shopping. It took a moment for the idea to sink in. "Uh, yeah," he said, trying to recover. "It's in the pocket of my jeans. I'll… I'll go get it." Bear started to rise from his seat.

"Sit down! Finish your breakfast! Have some more coffee and read the paper!" Griff ordered.

Bear picked up the Sports section while Griff perused the best-seller lists. Griff waited until Bear was absorbed in one of the columns on the Sports page before he spoke.

"So, do you think Cleveland will make it to the playoffs?"

"Not with most of their starting lineup on the injured list," said Bear. He picked up his coffee mug and was about to take a sip when he stopped and looked up at Griff, who was turning to the Fine Foods section. Bear stared for a moment then shrugged, sipped his coffee and looked over the previous night's final scores.

Griff finished his breakfast and carried his platter and flatware to the kitchen sink. He then headed to Bear's bedroom. "Which pocket?" he asked.

Bear looked up from the Sports page. "Oh, uh, front right."

Griff found the shopping list and barreled out the front door of the cave, still humming *Sweet Georgia Brown*.

"Ladies and gentlemen, it's Showtime!" he boomed to the crisp morning air as he cleared the doorway.

Bear cleared the table. As he put the dishes in the dishwasher, he watched Griff through the kitchen window. On grocery day Griff usually approached the edge of the cliff with all the enthusiasm of a chastised student on his way to the principal's office. This time he seemed to be pantomiming a basketball player driving in for a basket. He sent the imaginary basketball through an imaginary hoop and raised a clawed fist in a gesture of victory. And with that, he leapt off the cliff and disappeared.

Once more, Bear shrugged and shook his head. He made a sweep of the cave to look for more dirty dishes. As he collected Griff's teacup from the writing table, he noticed that Griff had put aside the latest Karolyne von Frankenburgh novel, *The Mayflower Griffin*. In the typewriter instead was a synopsis for a new story. While humming *Sweet Georgia Brown* (which was now firmly stuck in his head) Bear read the outline.

```
THE HOPSCOTCH DRAGON: A young griffin,
trembling with fear, warns the citizens
of two warring kingdoms that a dragon
twice his size is headed their way. A
truce is hastily forged and the two coun-
```

tries combine their forces to battle the
beast, only to discover that the dragon
wishes them to settle their differences
by playing hopscotch instead of going to
war. The dragon, having succeeded, bids
the citizens farewell and goes on his way,
meeting up later with the griffin, who had
earlier fled the scene in anticipation
of the dragon's arrival. The griffin and
the dragon, it turns out, are friends on
a mission to replace war with hopscotch.

Bear's eyes froze on the word "hopscotch" while the melody inside his head grew even more persistent.

"Oh, no!" he cried. "He wouldn't!"

Bear dressed quickly and ran out to the Suburban. He was about to climb behind the wheel when he realized he would have to break more than a few traffic laws to catch up to Griff.

He thought for a moment then walked around to the side of the cave and climbed a ladder to the loft he had built to pursue his interest in astronomy. After jotting down the angle, elevation and declination of the supernova he had sighted the previous night, Bear picked up the heavy telescope and carefully climbed down to the ground with it. He positioned the telescope at the edge of the cliff and affixed the terrestrial adapter. Then, starting at the high school where the guys were already playing basketball, he scanned up and down the street.

He spotted Griff at the intersection of Grahame Avenue and Shepard Drive, dribbling an invisible basketball while waiting for the WALK signal. When the signal changed, Griff crossed all six lanes of Grahame Avenue in just five griffin-sized steps.

CHAPTER 4

The Agony of Defeat

Griff strolled down the sidewalk and came to a stop outside the fifteen-foot-high fence that surrounded the basketball court. He crossed his arms on top of the fence, rested his head on his forelimbs and watched the action. The game moved toward the basket just inside the fence and one of the players executed a textbook layup. An opposing player threw the ball back into play from the sideline. He glanced up at Griff.

"What's up, big dude?" he said before dashing back onto the court.

"Mind if I join you?" asked Griff.

The players froze in place, as if an invisible referee had blown a silent whistle for a time-out. Everyone on the court and on the sidelines turned and looked at Griff. After an awkward moment of silence, Vance—one of the players—spoke up.

"Uh, Kyle's already keeping score, Griff."

Kyle, Vance's son, looked up from the oversized scorekeeper's book spread across his lap to wave at Griff.

"No, no," said Griff. "May I join the game?"

Vance looked around at the other players. "Anyone want to take a break?"

Kenny raised his hand and headed toward the bench. "My knee's acting up again."

"Okay, Griff's in for Kenny! You got that, Kyle?"

Kyle nodded.

Griff flapped his wings once for a little lift and swung himself over the fence.

"I've made a few changes to the rules to keep the competition fair," he said as he ambled to the center of the court. "I'll only shoot from outside the three-point line for two points and from center court for three. I'll also make free throws from center court, and the tallest player from the same team can substitute for me on jump balls. Is that okay?"

Vance and the other players shrugged and nodded in agreement.

"Sounds fair to me!" said Vance. "Play it in, big dude!"

Griff stepped outside the boundary line, bounced the ball back to Vance and joined the action on the court. Adhering to his own modified rules, he dribbled the ball outside of the three-point line before each shot. He even attempted a few from midcourt. Though Griff lacked the overall agility of his teammates, he made up for it with his reach and the accuracy of his shots, which seemed to improve as the game went on.

Watching through his telescope, Bear was impressed. "I never knew the big guy had it in him," he said to himself.

But as the game progressed and Griff's confidence increased, his ego ran away with him.

Bear watched as Griff caught a pass and held it in one claw, but instead of lobbing it at the hoop, Griff raised the ball over his head.

"No, Griff! Don't do it!" Bear yelled out loud.

"HE CAN LAY IT IN, BUT CAN HE SLAM IT?" Griff roared as he leapt into the air. He swung his arm in a wide arc toward the basket, but suddenly, he was teetering out of control.

The other players scrambled out of the way of Griff's tottering mass as he fell forward. Both the ball and his claw went through the hoop as he landed hard on his golden beak. The resulting smack echoed across the campus while the pole emitted a painful groan of wrenching metal and bent nearly in half.

Slightly stunned, Griff rose to his knees and tried to extract his claw from the hoop.

"Let go of the ball first, Griff," said Vance.

Dejected, Griff released the basketball. It bounced a few times on the asphalt and rolled away—as if it didn't want to be anywhere near him. He squeezed his talons together as tightly as he could and withdrew his claw from the twisted hoop. Then, without a word, he got to his feet and trudged to the fence.

"I'm sorry," he said quietly as he paused without looking back. "I didn't mean to make such a mess of things."

"Come back, Griff!" yelled Vance. "We can still play some half-court!"

Griff did not hear him. Embarrassed and humiliated, he hoisted himself over the fence and slunk down the street.

He wandered aimlessly in the general direction of the supermarket, until he found himself on the street where the girls were playing hopscotch. His mood perked up a little. He picked up a small stone. As he strolled down the sidewalk he tossed the stone into the air and caught it repeatedly.

"Is it my turn yet?" he asked as he approached the girls.

Just as before, the game stopped abruptly with every eye fixed on Griff.

"Do you really know how to play?" asked Julie.

"Ha! I was there when they invented the game!"

This was a bit of fanciful storytelling on Griff's part. He

was a mere seven hundred and forty-three years old; hopscotch dated back to ancient Rome.

Griff stepped confidently to the starting square and tossed his pebble; it landed a tad shy of the center. He raised his left foot, bounced slightly on his right foot and launched himself into the air. His right middle toe came down perfectly inside the second square, but before he could take his next hop, his foot plunged straight through the concrete, and the sidewalk swallowed him all the way up to his elbows.

"Well," he said wearily as the dust settled, "I think we can safely conclude that Goliath never played hopscotch."

He tried to free himself, but he was wedged so tightly that even with three girls tugging on each arm, he couldn't budge.

"I'll go get my Dad!" said Megan.

She and the rest of the girls darted off toward her father's hardware store.

Meanwhile, Griff rested his beak on a raised claw and drummed his talons on the sidewalk. He snapped to attention when Dennis came along.

"Fair warning, Dennis," Griff growled. "Before you ask what happened, let me remind you that I can turn a dragon inside out with these claws. Think of what I could do with just a single talon to a child barely nine years old. Now pick your words with care, young man… they may be the last you ever speak."

"What happened, Griff?" said Dennis.

Griff dropped the charade and cast his eyes toward the ground. "I was… I was trying to play hopscotch."

"*That* I can believe," said Dennis. He stared at Griff.

Griff stared back.

A full minute passed.

"Weren't you on your way home?" asked Griff.

"Nope."

"Aren't you on an errand for your mother? Won't she wonder why you're taking so long?"

"Nope."

"Don't you have somewhere else to be? *Anywhere* else?" Griff asked, kicking his voice up a few decibels.

Dennis shook his head. "I want to see how you get out of this."

A few minutes later, the hopscotch players returned with Megan's father, Stan. Stan carried an extra large can of aerosol lubricant.

"I don't think this is one of their 'Two Thousand and One Uses,' but if it works I'm going to send it in," he said with a chuckle.

Griff could only roll his chestnut-brown eyes.

Stan fitted the thin red extension tube into the sprayer nozzle. He walked around Griff and shot a few squirts of the lubricant between Griff and the concrete at intervals of an inch or two.

"Now hop up and down to work it in."

Griff gave him the most evil of evil eyes.

"Sorry," replied Stan.

Griff wiggled a little, and—much to his surprise—it seemed to work. With the girls pulling on his arms, Stan tugging his head in a headlock, and Dennis pushing against his back, Griff began to slide up and out of the concrete. When he was finally clear of the hole, he stood up and brushed himself off. His feathers and fur reeked of lubricant.

"Thank you, Stan," he said as he turned and walked away.

"Please tell the city maintenance department where to send the bill."

Griff headed off to the market with Dennis tagging along behind him.

After two complete disasters, the grocery shopping should be a picnic, he thought.

Up on the mountain, Bear had seen enough. He carried the telescope back to its perch and went inside to wait for Griff. Wisely, he began preparing one of Griff's favorite dishes, stuffed cabbage, even though it was Griff's turn to make dinner.

Griff and Dennis arrived at the supermarket.

"I can take it from here, Dennis," said Griff. He dropped to all fours and prepared for the difficult task of squeezing through the door.

"Can I push the cleanup cart for you?" asked Dennis.

Griff mulled over Dennis' offer. He smiled and nodded. Maybe the day was not a total loss after all.

"After you, Master Pearson."

Inside the supermarket, the odor of lubricant wafted through the air, and Griff had to endure remarks like, "What's that smell?" and, "Someone open a window!" But with Dennis mopping up after him, Griff finished the shopping much faster than usual.

Back at the city limits, Griff paused for a moment before taking to the air. "Thank you, Dennis. That meant a lot."

"Just living up to griffin's honor," Dennis replied. "Staring at you while you were stuck in the sidewalk was adding insult to injury. A griffin would never do that because if he did, he'd have to make things right or lose his wings."

"You may not be a griffin, Dennis, but you *are* a prince in the making. Good night, young sir."

Griff bowed and took off into the evening sky.

The aroma of dinner as he approached the cave made him glad he had another friend—a friend like Bear. Bear said nothing while Griff put away the groceries.

Feeling appreciative, Griff picked up his jug of horse shampoo and headed to a nearby mountain stream to scrub the odor out of his coat before dinner.

CHAPTER 5

"My Dinner with Bear"

Bear was already waiting at the dinner table when Griff returned from his bath and sat down to fill his plate with a half dozen cabbage rolls. Griff's fur and feathers were neatly groomed, and the chemical odor was gone. "Gee, Griff, what's the special occasion?" said Bear. "If I had known this was going to be a formal affair, I would have asked you to pick up my dinner jacket from the cleaners while you were in town today."

Griff managed half a grin as he tasted a cabbage roll. "Mmm... you remembered the paprika," he said attempting to dodge the question.

But Bear was not about to let him change the subject. "Why'd you do it, Griff?"

Griff knew better than to try and hide anything from Bear. Since he had spied on Bear, he certainly could not complain about Bear spying on him.

"I wanted them to like me the way they like you."

"They do," Bear assured him.

Griff shook his head. "No, they don't. I'm no good at basketball, and I can't even play a simple game of hopscotch without destroying half of Collinsfort Village."

"But you *didn't* destroy half the town. Think about it... if you asked me to read to a bunch of kids at the library I'd probably shake like a leaf and choke on my own tongue. Griff, they like you just as much as they like me, but for different reasons."

"Well, now they don't like me at all. I've gone and ruined everything," said Griff dejectedly.

"No, you haven't. You screwed up, but they'll fix the pole and the sidewalk, and in a couple of weeks no one will even remember."

"Yes, they will. I'm no better than a cheesy movie monster. If Hollywood calls, tell them I'll be happy to play the starring role in *Attack of the Creature with Two Left Feet.*"

"So, does this mean you're never going to set foot outside the cave again?"

"Of course not. I have obligations. I can't disappoint the children. I'll just have to come up with a way to get to the library without destroying the rest of the town."

Bear looked to Heaven for strength and gave up.

After dinner Griff put the dishes in the dishwasher, started it, and went back to his writing table. Bear was lying on the couch, riveted to the basketball game on the TV. Griff pulled the synopsis of *The Hopscotch Dragon* from the typewriter and inserted a clean sheet of paper. He had barely finished typing "The Griffin That Destroyed Chicago by Karolyne von Frankenburgh" when Bear yanked the paper from the machine.

He growled as he wadded up the sheet and hurled it into Griff's metal wastebasket, sending the bin somersaulting across the room. Then he reached up as high as he could, grabbed a paw full of Griff's chest feathers and hauled the startled griffin down to eye level.

"Try that again and I swear, I'll rip your typewriter apart with nothing but the claws God gave me. Do you understand?" he snarled with such ferocity that Griff felt it in his bones.

Griff nodded meekly.

"You are *not* a monster," Bear declared firmly. "You are a *griffin*. Griffins are noble creatures. They don't hurt people or destroy cities, and as long as you're living in *this* cave, Karolyne von Frankenburgh will not inflict a sorry excuse for a B-grade science fiction movie on her loyal readers!" He pushed Griff away so hard that the griffin nearly fell over on his back.

Griff recovered his balance and picked up the wastebasket. He shuddered, shaking loose a few feathers as he noticed a deep dent marking the spot where Bear's paper missile had struck the wastebasket. Since functioning IBM Selectric typewriters were rare, Griff prudently resumed work on *The Mayflower Griffin*.

The following Saturday Griff kept his appointment to read to the children, but instead of landing outside of town and walking the rest of the way, he flew directly to the library's courtyard and slipped quietly inside. He did not want to be seen if he could help it. Between story days at the library, Griff had become a hermit.

Bear found out on his next shopping trip just how much the people in town missed Griff's company. At the basketball court, Jeff told him that Griff had not been visiting his espresso stand. He had not been to the library during the week either, according to Larry, the town's assistant librarian. Since Griff no longer walked to the library on Saturdays, all of the brightly colored "Follow the Griffin!" posters advertising his story time had been taken down.

The hopscotch players told Bear that Griff had been reading stories with sad endings instead of his usual choice of humorous tales and stirring epics. He had even managed to turn a lighthearted yarn like *The Griffin and the Minor Canon* into a three-hankie tearjerker. Bear was so worried about Griff that he committed two fouls while playing regulation hopscotch and added thirteen seconds to his time when he tried to beat Megan's Fancy-Foot record.

"I'm really off my game today," he lamented as he climbed back into the Suburban. He stared at the dashboard for a while and was about to start the engine when he had an idea. He jumped out of the SUV and ran back to tell the hopscotch players.

"Yeah, we can do that," said Julie. "How much will we need?"

"As much as you can get your hands on," said Bear. "And in as many colors as you can find."

Bear slid into the SUV and hurried back to the basketball court where the game was still in progress. The players took a short time-out to listen to Bear's proposal and agreed to give it a try.

"Hey, one week out of eight without basketball won't kill us," said Vance.

Bear thanked them and hopped back into the Suburban. When he arrived at the market, he asked to see the store manager.

Earl thought over Bear's plan. "It's going to take a lot of work, Bear."

"I know, but isn't Griff one of your best customers? He could take his business to any of the big chains in Fort Collins, but he trusts you, Earl. He knows you'll stock what he wants. A griffin's trust isn't something just anyone can earn."

"Well, he did clear the street in front of the market a few

42

winters ago when the snowplow broke down. I guess we never thanked him properly for that."

"So you'll do it?"

"You know I will, Bear."

Bear finished the grocery shopping and steered the Suburban to the park. He felt good about what he had just done and was ready for a reward from Vinnie's Ice Cream Chalet.

"Vinnie! The Bear's in the mood for a Bear Trap!" he bellowed as he stepped up to the counter.

Vinnie chuckled and went right to work, splitting two bananas and arranging them in a large plastic bowl so they resembled the gaping jaws of a bear trap.

"Name your bait, Bear."

"Espresso bean, mocha almond fudge and rocky road on both sides. And don't spare the hot fudge or whipped cream."

Bear sat down on a vacant bench outside the shop and plowed into the ice cream creation Vinnie had named after him. Across the footpath sat Dennis, fully absorbed in a copy of *Sinister Symphony*, the latest Karolyne von Frankenburgh novel.

Dennis happened to glance in Bear's direction as he turned the page. His blue eyes grew as big as CDs. Using the book as a shield, he watched Bear's every move.

Bear finished his sundae and stood up. He nodded to Dennis as he deposited the empty bowl in a nearby trash can. Then, recalling a particularly corny chapter in *Sinister Symphony,* he began laughing to himself as he headed back to the Suburban.

He's playing games with my mind, thought Dennis wildly. *I can't take it anymore!*

He closed the book, rose to his feet and planted himself in the middle of the footpath. "I know everything about you, Bear!" he shouted.

Bear stopped and turned around.

"Dennis?"

"You're the real Karolyne von Frankenburgh! Don't even try to deny it!"

Dennis dropped his book and went into a frenzied dance, orbiting Bear and pointing at him.

"The secret's out! Look, everyone! It's Karolyne von Frankenburgh! Ask him for her autograph! Bear is Karolyne von Frankenburgh!"

The park's other visitors glanced toward the commotion then went about their business shaking their heads in bewilderment. Bear stared at Dennis until the two made eye contact. Seeing Bear's gaze, Dennis froze, dropped to his knees and burst into tears.

Bear crouched down next to him. "Why are you crying, Dennis?"

"Because now you're going to kill me, and Griff's going to kill you!" Dennis wailed. "And then he's going to carry away what's left of me in a bucket."

Bear nodded slowly, his eyes narrowing. "Right." He picked up the book and helped Dennis back to the bench. "Trust me, Dennis; I'm not going to kill anybody—especially you. Now, tell me where you heard such a ridiculous thing."

Dennis explained how he had found the royalty statement from Chrestus & Minos, how he had spied on Bear in the post office and then later reported what he had observed to Griff.

Bear snorted a growl through his nose causing Dennis to cringe.

"I'm not mad at you, Dennis." Bear glanced in the direction of the cave. "I'm mad at a giant skunk in a griffin suit who writes books under a name that's so phony it wouldn't fool your Uncle Fritz in Heidelberg."

Dennis giggled. He had never heard Griff described that way.

Bear turned back to Dennis.

"You're not entirely off the hook. It sounds like Griff tried to tell you the truth, but you still jumped to conclusions about me. Don't you know me better than that?"

"Yes, I do," said Dennis. "I'm sorry."

"Still, Griff should have known better, too. He's a lot older than you. Heck, he's a lot older than nearly everyone on the planet."

Bear paused. A sly grin began to spread over his face, making him look more like an oversized fox than a bear. He started to chortle until the bench quaked from his laughter. "I think we should teach Griff a lesson," he said.

"How?" asked Dennis.

"Well, Griff said I'm going to kill you, right?"

Dennis nodded.

Bear smiled as he handed Dennis a cell phone. "Call your mother and ask her if you can come to the cave for dinner a month from today. You like spaghetti and meatballs, don't you?"

Dennis looked a bit confused, but he nodded as he dialed the phone.

"Good!" exclaimed Bear. "Before we have dinner, we're going to roast a griffin and smother him in ketchup... *lots and lots of ketchup.*"

CHAPTER 6

The End of a Perfect Day

It was once again the last Saturday of the month, and again Bear woke up smelling coffee. As he pulled on his bathrobe he had a feeling he would find Griff in the kitchen, but this time not making wild blueberry pancakes. To save himself a trip back to the bedroom, he fished the shopping list out of his jeans and slipped it into his bathrobe pocket as he headed out to the kitchen.

Griff was sitting at the kitchen table reading the newspaper. He had already finished his breakfast and was looking over the best-seller lists. From the way he arched his eyebrows as he read, Bear knew that another of Karolyne von Frankenburgh's sagas had been added to the Fantasy/Sci-Fi section of the list. The bruin poured himself a mug of coffee and sat down at the table where Griff had set out the Cocoa Grenades and Bear's cereal bowl.

"Can we get this over with as quickly as possible?" said Griff without looking up from the paper.

Bear pulled out the shopping list and slid it across the table, leaving it near the coupons Griff had stacked next to his huge coffee mug.

"They miss you, Griff," said Bear filling his bowl with cereal.

"I'm sure they do," said Griff. He put the shopping list and the coupons in his wallet. "They miss seeing me make a fool of myself."

"No, Griff, they miss *you*. You know, not every town has its own resident griffin. They're waiting for you."

"Probably waiting to stuff me and turn me into the next exhibit at the Museum of Natural History. I'd better mention in my will that I'd rather be put on display at the library or I'll wind up between the polar bear and that spotted hyena with the goofy grin."

"We both know that's not going to happen, Griff."

Bear was right of course, but in a moment like this, Griff was not sure whether to give him a big manly bear hug or squash him like a big brown furry insect just for being so right. Instead he simply decided to maintain an air of indifference. He rose silently and dramatically, carried his breakfast dishes to the sink and left.

Through the window Bear watched Griff approach the cliff with his usual lack of enthusiasm. Griff took a deep breath, closed his eyes and flung himself into empty space.

A sinister grin replaced Bear's normally placid appearance. "Enjoy it while you can, you big buzzard," he sneered. He finished his breakfast, dressed and started a batch of spaghetti sauce with meatballs in the slow cooker.

Meanwhile, Griff landed in town. He stared for a minute or two at the "Welcome to Collinsfort Village" arch that straddled the road.

"If I come home plucked and skinned, it's *your* fault!" he called in the general direction of the cave and his roommate. Then, in his most regal gait, he strode down Main Street.

The people who passed him on the sidewalk behaved as

if he had never been gone, tossing off their usual greetings of, "Hey, Griff!" and, "How's it goin', Griff?"

He had gone about four blocks when he realized with relief that no one intended to pelt him with eggs or rotten tomatoes. Still, he wasn't completely convinced that he was out of the woods.

At the corner of Main Street and Grahame Avenue he glanced in the window of the Village Book Nook. The shopkeeper was setting up a display that included Karolyne von Frankenburgh's newly listed best-seller. Griff paused, pretending to study the book. The intersection of Grahame and Shepard loomed in the distance. The shopkeeper noticed Griff and waved. Griff waved back then hurried along, concealing his reluctance as best he could. At the intersection, he stopped for the DON'T WALK signal. It changed to WALK far too quickly.

As he crossed Grahame Avenue, his ears were trained on the basketball courts at Collinsfort Village High School. To his surprise, he didn't hear anyone playing ball. More curious than hesitant now, he approached the basketball court and saw the players sitting on the sidelines. They appeared to be deep in thought. Pretending not to notice them, Griff continued down the sidewalk.

"Hey, Griff!" yelled Vance. "Get over here, man! We need one more!"

"One more for what?" asked Griff swinging himself over the fence.

The players were paired up around several chessboards. Vance was the odd man out, still waiting for an opponent.

"Well, this hardly seems fair," said Griff.

"It's okay, I'll teach you how to play," said Vance.

"No, no, I mean, it's hardly fair for me to play against one of you at a time."

"Well, how else do you play chess?"

"How about, I play against all of you at once?"

Vance grinned. "This I've got to see."

As the high school's gym coach and computer science teacher, Vance had keys to the equipment and supply rooms. He brought out four more chessboards, and Griff lined them up on the bench. The nine basketball players each sat down next to a chessboard.

"Players Two, Four, Six and Eight, please turn your boards around and play white," said Griff. "Playing both sides keeps me on my toes."

Griff walked up and down the row of chessboards, making white's opening move on five of the boards and black's countermove on the rest. As the multiple games proceeded, Griff broke the silence with little comments and remarks.

"Budapest 1953 all over again… now, *that's* one I haven't seen in a while. Boris Spassky in disguise, maybe? Ooh, that's *got* to hurt!"

An hour later, Griff had checkmated seven of his opponents, been defeated by another, and had ended one game in a stalemate.

"I'm a bit out of practice," he said. "Next time, gentlemen?"

"Yeah, sure! That was great!"

"Man, I need some practice myself!"

Griff felt much better than he had an hour ago. He leaped over the fence and continued down the street. "Thank you, Bear," he whispered.

He headed directly to the street where the girls played hopscotch to see what else Bear had been up to. As he suspected, the girls were not playing hopscotch. Instead, they were on their hands and knees creating chalk drawings on the sidewalk. They looked up from their work only long enough to say, "Hi, Griff!"

Griff saw an unopened box of colored chalk lying next to a vacant patch of sidewalk. "Well, when in Rome…" he said as he hunkered down next to the concrete.

He took out a stick of chalk and hummed a little Verdi as the color swooped across the improvised cement canvas. He switched from one color to another, alternating between long sweeping strokes and minute details. Half an hour later, he stood up and clapped his claws together to shake off the chalk dust.

"There!" he announced.

The girls stood up from their drawings of ducks, bunnies, kitties and puppies to gather around Griff's museum-quality rendition of Leonardo da Vinci's *Mona Lisa*.

"Next time: *The Last Supper*!" Griff said as he headed to the supermarket.

For the rest of the day, the girls diverted foot traffic around the chalk *Mona Lisa* while people hurried home to get their cameras.

Meanwhile, Griff nearly walked past the supermarket's parking lot. It had been completely taken over by an immense circus tent. A banner on the tent proclaimed "TENTLOAD OF SAVINGS!" The main tent flap was tied back to its full width, and Griff—curious as any griffin worth his wings would be—stepped inside to have a look around.

The tent was so tall that Griff could stand upright. Several aisles had been set up far enough apart that Griff could walk between them without his wings knocking bottles, cartons or jars off the shelves. The store employees were all dressed as circus performers. Earl played the part of the impresario. He stood inside the circus tent's center ring and barked into a megaphone, "Hurry, hurry, hurry, one and all! See the amazing tumbling prices! Marvel at the incredible growing savings! Watch in wonder as we tame your wild, runaway food budget!"

Griff took a shopping cart and was relieved when no one chased him down with that wretched cleanup cart. He unfolded the shopping list and was amazed to find that every item on the paper was available in the big, roomy circus tent. He took his time, savoring the marvelous sensation of walking upright as he shopped.

When he was finished, he pushed his cart to the cash register near the tent door. Mark, the cashier, was dressed in a lion costume.

"So, Dad," said Griff as he unloaded his groceries, "when are they going to make you store manager?"

Mark didn't miss a beat. "Next spring, son, when your mother flies north again."

"Touché!" said Griff.

He carried his shopping bags back to the city limits, spread his mighty wings and rose into the air. When he had climbed to the height of the cave, he turned to take one more look at the town. Though he lived in the cave on the mountain, he realized that Collinsfort Village was very much his home.

Griff knew what he had to do next. His instincts had always told him that Dennis could be trusted with Fräulein von Frankenburgh's secret. He really should have followed those instincts. He felt bad about using Bear and Dennis the way he had; he vowed that at the first opportunity, he would confess what he had done and ask their forgiveness. Just thinking about it made him feel all warm inside.

However, that warm, cozy feeling did not last long. Griff landed and sensed at once that something was not right. Bear should have been waxing the Suburban, but his can of car wax, gym sock applicators and diaper buffing cloths were strewn all around the Suburban, as if he had hastily abandoned the task. From around the side of the cave came the sound of soft weeping. Griff dropped the bags and rushed to investigate.

Bear sat in a trembling heap against the cave wall staring at his claws and weeping. In front of him lay Dennis—not moving at all, save for his brown hair which rustled in the midday breeze. Bear's teeth and claws, and Dennis' throat were bathed in oozing, glistening red. Dennis' motionless hand clutched a rumpled sheet of paper. On it he had drawn a lifelike image of Bear seated at a computer, typing furiously in front of a bookcase bulging with the works of Karolyne von Frankenburgh.

Bear looked up at Griff. "See what you made me do?" he said through his tears.

Griff was stunned.

"*Me*? How did *I* make you do *this*?"

Bear tugged the picture from Dennis' grasp and held it in his lap. "I promised I'd keep your secret—no matter what—but Dennis told me everything. There was no other way, Griff. I had to tell him the real story, and then…." He shifted his gaze to Dennis.

Suddenly his voice was solemn. "Now, Griff. Do it now while I'm not looking. Make it quick and painless, like the way the griffin wrung the life out of that Bengal tiger in *Menagerie of Mayhem*; I don't want to feel a thing. Ohh, I hope Dennis didn't feel it, but the last thing he saw couldn't have been pretty."

Griff knelt beside his friend. "I never meant for things to get this far out of hand, Bear. I'm a selfish pig, a weasel masquerading as a noble griffin. I let my privacy become the most important thing in my life, even more important than life itself—and Dennis' life, at that. I'm the one who should pay for this, not you. My life for his, and it can't be by my own hand; that would be the coward's way out. You can tell the authorities that I did this to Dennis, and when I came at you to silence the only witness to the crime, you overpowered me. It was self-defense on your part."

Bear laid the drawing near Dennis' hand. "A little boy is one thing, Griff, but you were built to slay dragons. You can fight off a whole pride of lions and not lose a single feather. Who's going to believe one bear could bring down a griffin?"

"If I pull back my feathers and show you exactly where my jugular is located, you'll only need one swift bite."

"And then what?" said Bear. "We keep piling one lie on top of another? If you take the rap for me, I'll spend the rest of my life knowing I'm the reason my two best friends are gone. I can't go on hiding the truth from the world. That's no way to live. Just finish me so the lying can stop."

"No! A griffin's honor demands *my* life," Griff declared. He threw himself on the ground, closed his eyes, and exposed the most vulnerable part of his throat. "Bear, I hold you blameless for what you are about to do. A debt like this can be paid no other way."

A small voice interrupted the drama. "Excuse me, will whoever is left standing please bring back some French fries?"

Griff leaped to his feet and staggered backward as if Dennis were glowing with radiation. Then, tripping over his own tail, he landed flat on his back with his wings splayed out on both sides.

Bear collapsed into a fetal position. He was laughing so hard he couldn't stand up for nearly two minutes.

Dennis sat up. He dragged a finger through the puddle of red trickling down his shirt and licked it off. "Mmm, the best-selling ketchup in America. Wouldn't you hate to see it go to waste, Griff?"

Griff picked himself up off the ground, but seething with rage, he was unable to form a coherent sentence. He snatched up the shopping bags and stormed into the cave without a word, while Dennis and Bear—still laughing—cleaned up.

An hour later they all sat down to dinner, and over Bear's spaghetti and quarter-pound meatballs, everything was finally straightened out. By the time Bear brought the spumoni to the table, one more person in the world knew Karolyne von Frankenburgh's true identity, and all was forgiven.

Later that evening after Dennis' mother picked him up, Griff sat at his writing table. *The Mayflower Griffin* was complete and already on its way to the publisher.

"Karolyne, my dear, I think you've caused enough trouble for now," said Griff out loud.

"What was that?" asked Bear as he loaded the dishwasher.

"Oh, nothing." Griff rolled a clean sheet of paper into the Selectric.

Bear wandered over to have a look as Griff typed out the title of his next project.

```
The Greatest Chess Matches
   of the Past 500 Years:
  An Eyewitness Account
by Errington Felzworth Griffin
```

"Griff, that's not your pen name," said Bear.

"I know," said Griff, crossing his arms and looking at the byline with a smile. "I've never been to a book signing before; I think it's time to find out what it's like."

Two Years Later

CHAPTER 7

Last Stop on the Book Tour

"Welcome back," said Jay Leno. "Just a reminder, Howie Mandel is appearing at Caesar's Tahoe through the end of the month and Kelsey Grammer, of course, we see every day in his two hit TV series, both in syndication.

"Our next guest sat down at his typewriter two years ago, and he didn't get up until he had crammed five hundred years of history into three hundred and seventy-five pages, which is a little like stuffing a horse into a gym bag. And believe me... he's big enough to do *that*, too. The author of the *New York Times* best-seller *The Greatest Chess Matches of the Past 500 Years: An Eyewitness Account*—from Collinsfort Village, Colorado, let's welcome Errington Felzworth Griffin."

The band launched into a jazzed-up arrangement of the Masterpiece Theater theme. A stagehand pulled back one half of the curtain. Griff carefully swept back the other half and strode onto the soundstage to the enthusiastic applause of the audience. His wings barely cleared the overhead lighting grid as he stepped to the edge of the stage and bowed gracefully, looming over the first several rows of seats. He straightened up and walked to the bottom of the small elevated platform at the left end of the stage while Howie, Kelsey and Jay rose to their feet.

After exchanging handshakes, the men returned to their seats, and Griff stepped onto a large oval rug that had been spread out on the floor to the right of the platform. He bowed to the audience once more, sat down on the rug and leaned toward Jay's desk, resting his elbow on the top step of the platform.

"Boy, when you make an entrance…" said Jay.

"One can't be subtle when one is twenty feet tall, I suppose," said Griff, setting off a ripple of laughter and a sprinkle of applause from the audience. "And do call me Griff."

"Now, Griff, your book is about chess, but readers of all ages are buying it as if it were the latest from Stephen King or John Grisham. Any idea why?"

"I haven't the foggiest, but I'm certainly not going to complain."

"The first two weeks it was on the *Times* best-seller list, they put it with the myth and legend books."

"Yes, that was a little embarrassing. For a while, many readers thought it was a book *about* a griffin, not *by* one."

Leno grinned at the audience and winked. "Like one of Karolyne von Frankenburgh's novels?"

Griff rolled his eyes and feigned contempt at the mere mention of the name. "Oh, please," he said, turning up his beak. "It's only a coincidence that she and I have the same publisher."

Bear tried in vain to hold back a snicker. He sat in the VIP section of the studio audience along with Howie and Kelsey's invited guests.

"It covers five hundred years of chess history, and you call it an eyewitness account," said Jay. "Mind if I ask how old you are?"

"Not at all. I'm seven hundred and forty-five years old."

The audience gasped and murmured while Kelsey piped

up, "You know, you don't look a day over five hundred and eighty-two."

"Well, I do keep a birthday candle factory running around the clock," Griff shot back with perfect comic timing.

The audience broke into a wave of laughter while Griff glanced at Bear. Bear had come up with the one-liner years earlier, and Griff was glad to get a chance to use it, especially on network TV!

"So, the two years it took you to write the book probably flew by," said Jay.

"Actually, writing and revising the manuscript took six months of full-time work. Then the publisher needed another eighteen months to edit the manuscript, print the books and ship them out to the stores. And no, time doesn't fly when you're waiting to see your name on the cover of your first book—no matter how old you are."

"What's the most memorable game in the book?" asked Jay.

Griff rested his beak on his raised claw and gazed up into the lights for a moment.

"Hmmm… Bucharest, 1653. Arno Przlevski and Ignatz Svjataslov wagered their summer estates on the game. Przlevski proceeded to checkmate Svjataslov in a mere seven moves."

"Whoa! I gather Svjataslov was upset?"

"A tad. At the banquet following the match, Svjataslov toasted Przlevski, congratulated him on his victory, and wished him many happy summers at his new holiday house. Przlevski took one nip of his wine and keeled over dead."

"He was *poisoned*?"

"Well, Svjataslov never was a gracious loser."

"And you were there?"

Griff nodded. "I was seated at the banquet table opposite Przlevski. The spilled wine left a stain on my coat that didn't come out for two weeks. We didn't have spot remover in those days, you know."

Jay shook his head in amazement as the band chimed a time cue. He turned to the close-up camera and held up a copy of Griff's book. "The book is *The Greatest Chess Matches of the Past 500 Years: An Eyewitness Account* by Errington Felzworth Griffin, published by Chrestus & Minos. Griff will be signing it tomorrow at Noble's Book Barn in Century City. We'll be back right after this."

"And we're clear," said the stage manager.

Jay picked up a pen and turned to Griff. "Would you do me the honor, Griff?"

Griff nodded and grinned. On the overleaf he wrote:

To the man who keeps America up past its bedtime,
All the best!
E. F. Griffin

With a few deft strokes of the pen, he added a tiny drawing of a smiling griffin. He handed the book and the pen back just as the stage manager announced, "Back in five... four... three... two..."

The band struck up the closing credits theme.

"Howie Mandel, Caesar's Tahoe! Kelsey Grammer, every day on *Cheers* and *Frasier*! And you can meet Errington Felzworth Griffin in person at Noble's Book Barn in Century City tomorrow! Good night!"

Jay waved to the cheering crowd as the cameras panned back and faded.

Griff exited the studio through one of the oversized equipment doors, but that didn't stop a small pack of book-wielding autograph hounds from hunting him down. Cornered (and relishing every moment of it), Griff reached for the first book while his fans formed a loose single-file line.

"Catch up to me at the hotel!" said Bear as he strolled past on his way to a rented Chevy Suburban.

Griff patiently signed every book he was handed. After autographing the last one he stood up and sauntered over to a helicopter pad painted on the asphalt.

"FAA rules," he joked while spreading his mighty wings. He ascended into the air above Burbank and followed the contour of the 405 Freeway back to the hotel where he walked, barely noticed, though the main lobby. Since he was far too big for any of the hotel's rooms, or even a suite, the hotel staff had made up the biggest ballroom to accommodate him, including a fresh pile of straw instead of a bed.

The message lamp on the speakerphone was blinking. Griff perched his reading glasses on his beak so he could read the tiny instructions on the phone. He pressed the speaker bar, followed by the button marked Messages.

A woman's recorded voice came on the line. "You have... one... new message, from... the guest in room... two... one... seven." The next voice Griff heard was Bear's.

"Sorry, Griff, but I called Hamburger Hamlet. They don't have an outdoor dining area, but they do have a 'to go' menu, though the food might not be as warm as you like when it gets here. Looks like you'll have to choke down room service again at your publisher's expense. Yeah, I know, it's a cushy job but someone's gotta do it. I've got an early plane to catch, so I'm turning in right after dinner. Say 'Hi' to your friend in Santa Barbara for me. See you back at the cave!"

"There are no more messages," said the recorded voice.

Griff hung up the phone and picked up the room service menu. He perused it for a minute or two then pressed the speaker bar once more, followed by the room service button.

"Room service. This is Todd. It's my pleasure to serve you. What would you like, Mr. Griffin?"

"I'll have the Cajun blackened swordfish—a double portion—with a double side of the seafood jambalaya, and can you make that extra spicy?"

"We most certainly can! Anything else?"

"Uh, a pot of coffee and three slices of the pecan praline cheesecake for dessert."

"Very good! That should be up in thirty to forty-five minutes."

"Thank you," said Griff.

He switched off the speakerphone, picked up a remote control and tuned the big screen TV to the NBC affiliate in Los Angeles. During the *Channel 4 News*, a commercial spot for *The Tonight Show* aired.

"Howie Mandel, Kelsey Grammer and an author you've got to *see* to believe, all tonight!" said Jay Leno, at a pace that likely broke the world speed-talking record.

By the time room service brought Griff's dinner, three more spots had aired. In the last of the three, Jay Leno described Griff as "an author who's as big as his book's sales figures!"

Griff rolled his eyes and shook his head. "I have a name, Jay," he muttered.

After dinner, Griff pushed the room service cart out of the ballroom and hung the DO NOT DISTURB tag on the doorknob.

He settled into the pile of straw and propped himself up

enough to see the TV between his toes. He had trouble understanding the attraction of prime time television; most of his evenings were spent writing. It was going to be a long three hours until *The Tonight Show* broadcast.

CHAPTER 8

"Here There Be Dragons"

Thanks to Griff's TV appearance, the crowd at Noble's Book Barn was much larger than expected, and the book signing had to be extended by an hour. Griff had anticipated this and informed his friend Dorian that his arrival in Santa Barbara might be delayed. By one o'clock, he had chatted with each of his admirers, signed their books and thanked the bookstore staff.

Griff was especially grateful that Noble's Book Barn—like the library back home—was large enough to let him sign books inside the store. At other stops on the tour, Griff had been forced to sit in the main corridor of shopping malls with the tips of his jackal ears visible to shoppers on the upper level. He had politely turned down requests from autograph seekers who leaned precariously over the railing; he advised them to wait their turn in line on the lower level. To his refined nature it had all been rather disconcerting.

But now, with it all behind him, Griff flew toward the ocean and turned north along Pacific Coast Highway. Dorian's directions took Griff to a small seaside airport, which explained Dorian's somewhat cryptic address of 2330 Airport Service Road.

Griff touched down and strolled past a line of bland gray and beige hangars until he came to one that stood out from the others—a hangar wrapped completely in a colorful forty-foot high montage. The montage depicted a bustling community with a busy airport; a boardwalk with carousel, wooden roller coaster and Ferris wheel; surfers riding the waves; and a large begoggled golden eagle who swooped over a lush vineyard with a tiny goggle-wearing rabbit riding on his back clutching a bunch of grapes. In the blue sky over the airport scene, the artist had painted in neat white lettering:

HERE THERE BE DRAGONS DORIAN

Griff raised an eyebrow at the words, then headed for the entrance. Apparently Dorian entertained human-sized visitors more often than griffins; the doorbell was located only four feet off the ground. Griff stooped down and pressed the tiny push button next to the hangar's tall double doors.

From within the hangar, Griff could hear the gentle thump of Dorian's long footsteps approaching the door. A pair of electric motors powered up and the hangar's doors began to part.

The first thing to meet Griff's eyes was a button the size of a dinner plate. It was attached to the bottom of a fabric and leather vest encircling an expansive reptilian torso. Tipping his head back, Griff counted two more enormous buttons before his eyes finally made contact with Dorian's.

"Here there be dragons!" exclaimed Griff, throwing open his arms.

"Erry!" cried Dorian, calling Griff by a nickname he had not heard in, well, centuries. Griff stood as tall as he could without rising on tiptoes, while Dorian dropped to his knees and wrapped Griff in a warm, genuine embrace of friendship. As large as Griff was, he could barely bring his claws together around Dorian's broad neck.

There was a time many centuries ago when a griffin and a dragon standing this close together would have been trying to tear each other limb from limb. But that was in the past. Now the two friends parted and stepped back to get a full-length view of each other. Dorian's scales were still the same iridescent shade of green-tinged blue that Griff remembered. Unlike many cartoon depictions of his kind, Dorian did not have a light colored ribbed belly patch running from his chin to the underside of his tail. He was also not the oversized pot-bellied pixie with smoking nostrils that lurked inside so many children's storybooks nor the muscle-bound, red-eyed embodiment of fire-breathing evil found in comic books.

He could best be described as a winged lizard standing upright. He had muscular legs for leaping into the air as he took flight, and his great tail acted as a rudder to stabilize him on the ground. Despite being folded, the prismatic membranes of his wings refracted traces of sunlight into tiny rainbows on the pavement. In flight, those wings could cast rainbows over entire city blocks while the canards on each side of his head threw their own miniature shimmering prisms.

Dorian dropped to one knee again and framed Griff between his fingers. With one eye closed, he peered through the imaginary viewfinder and smiled, revealing a mouthful of long, sharp daggerlike teeth.

"You look just like you did on TV last night!" he proclaimed, standing up. "And what's this 'You may call me Griff' business, Erry?"

"I prefer Griff; it sounds less *airy* than Erry."

Dorian tried a few inflections on for size. "Griff... *GRIFF...* GrrrrrIFF! Hmmm... makes you sound tougher than you really are."

"Well, we could always go back to calling you Dory."

"Not if you want to leave Santa Barbara in one piece... *Griff.*"

"You're welcome," said Griff in a deliberate non sequitur.

"Oh, no!" cried Dorian. "Monique!"

"Monique?"

"My model! I forgot all about her!"

Dorian headed back inside the hangar with Griff in tow. Cans of paint sat on the shelves that lined one wall. They were arranged by the hues of the white light spectrum, starting with shades of red, then orange, yellow, green, blue, indigo and finally, violet. In one corner of the hangar was evidence that an artist had been at work. Several sheets of butcher paper were taped to the wall and covered with rough sketches and detailed studies. An assortment of paintbrushes and other implements sat nearby on a scaffold that served as a table for Dorian.

Under a quartet of floodlights a woman with long brown hair sat on a small raised platform. She wore a gauze gown and a white linen toga. Next to her lay a prop bow and arrow.

"Please forgive me, Monique! If you can remember the last pose, we'll be finished in fifteen minutes," said Dorian, picking up a charcoal stick. He positioned himself in front of the sheet of butcher paper on which he had begun a sketch of Monique.

Monique rose to her feet and picked up the props. "I think I was looking over at the—" Her voice abruptly rose to an ear-shattering shriek as she dropped the bow and arrow.

The scream reverberated in Griff's sensitive ears, making him leap into the air with a start.

Dorian looked first at Monique and then turned to see what had frightened her. There in her line of sight stood Griff, with a few of his feathers flitting to the floor.

"Oh, uh, Monique, this is Griff, a friend of mine from Colorado. Griff, Monique—my model for Diana, goddess of the hunt."

Griff stepped forward and held out his claw for a hand-shake. Monique snatched up the bow and arrow, and wielded them in self-defense.

Griff sensed the tension in the room. "I'll wait over there until you're finished," he said, retreating to a remote corner of Dorian's studio. But even that did not seem to help. "On second thought, I'm going outside to watch the planes take off and land."

Sometime later, Griff had counted five Lear corporate jets and three Embraer Brasilia commuter planes as he sat against the wall of the building. Finally, the hangar doors began to slide open. Griff turned and looked up. He expected to see Dorian looming over him.

"I'm so sorry," said a woman's voice. Griff looked down and saw Monique, now wearing a pair of jeans and a crepe shirt and carrying a canvas harbor bag. "Dorian's visitors usually aren't so..."

"Tall and handsome?" said Griff, rising to his feet.

Monique laughed. "I know. It was silly." She held out her hand, and Griff gently shook it. "I'm posing in front of someone who's big enough to be Godzilla's understudy, and I practically lose it over a..."

"A griffin," said Griff with a hint of a courtly bow.

"Yes, a griffin half his size. And you want to know what's even sillier?"

"What's that?"

"I saw you on *The Tonight Show* last night! I should have recognized you!" Monique reached into her bag and pulled out a copy of Griff's book, along with a pen. "You're not *too* mad at me, are you?" she asked.

Griff chuckled and shook his head as he took the pen from Monique. He sat down and braced the book against his knee. "To Monique?"

She nodded.

Griff handed back the signed book and watched while Monique climbed into her car. Then he wandered back inside.

Dorian had turned the sketch of Monique around and was rubbing charcoal over the entire reverse side.

"Still drawing murals?" asked Griff.

"Yep. There isn't a museum big enough for what I paint these days," replied Dorian with a grin. "This one's for the outside wall of the university's new amphitheater. By the way, how's Karolyne?"

"She's fine. She was causing trouble so I sent her away on a short vacation, though I'm tempted to put her in a convent and leave her there for the rest of her life."

"That's good, but the next time you see her, can you ask her one little question?" said Dorian.

"And that is…?"

"Why does the dragon always have to die?" said Dorian, covering the last few inches of the paper with charcoal. He put down the charcoal and picked up a bed sheet, which he used as a rag to wipe the charcoal from his claws.

Griff shrugged. "It sells books. Besides, the dragon didn't die in *Prince of the Sky*."

Dorian stopped wiping and narrowed his eyes. "That's because he was a prince under a wizard's spell, not a real dragon!"

"But he didn't die, *and* he won the heart of the beautiful princess, *and* they lived happily ever after… the end," said Griff with a mischievous grin.

Dorian shook his head and tossed the sheet aside. "Feel like a walk before dinner?"

"Sounds wonderful."

Dorian opened the hangar doors all the way to a sweeping view of Santa Barbara.

"Welcome to my gallery," he said.

CHAPTER 9

A Tour of the Gallery and Dinner by the Sea

Dorian had settled in Santa Barbara in the early 1930s. He had found Hollywood too gaudy and San Francisco too snooty (an art critic dismissed his only San Francisco mural as "a cute trick, but then, King Kong could have done as well, given the proper training"). Here, despite his towering height, he blended perfectly into Santa Barbara's artistic community and had become an immediate sensation for his ability to create vast murals without elaborate scaffolding that cluttered the sidewalk.

Both Dorian and Griff had acquired a sixth sense that allowed them to slip instinctively under utility lines as they strolled the streets of Santa Barbara. Dorian carried his tail aloft like a Tyrannosaurus Rex, and when he turned a corner, his tail followed the contour of the turn instead of swinging out and becoming a hazard to busses, trucks or other high-profile vehicles. The citizens had grown so used to Dorian that they knew his stride and gait. They walked around his feet and strolled between his legs as easily as if he were part of the sidewalk. Griff, in contrast, had to dodge the pedestrians who were unaccustomed to his presence.

Dorian's gallery was the entire city, always open to the public with no admission fee. One needed only to look for his unique DdiD monogram (for Dorian di Drago) to find one of his murals.

73

"I painted this for the head chef's grandfather," he said, pointing out a reproduction of a Monet on the outside wall of a French restaurant. The mural was as vibrant as the day it was first painted. Dorian's fee included lifetime maintenance, and he still had a few good centuries left in him.

A nearby Catholic church displayed a gigantic portrait of the Pope elevating the Holy Eucharist at the moment of Consecration. Dorian had chosen the hues so carefully that the Pontiff appeared to be lit by heavenly rays in the same shade as the sunshine falling on the sidewalk.

The Old Santa Barbara shopping district was home to a palatial movie theater that showed classic films. The theater was adorned with an immense painted "poster" of Al Jolson advertising for all time the premiere of *The Jazz Singer*. "Stare at him long enough," joked Dorian, "and you'll hear him say, 'Wait a minute, you ain't heard nothin' yet!'"

The local Subaru dealership was something of a time machine. While the latest models were displayed in the floor-to-ceiling window facing the street, the entire wall opposite afforded a peek into the past, with a hippie-looking man and woman contemplating the purchase of a tiny jelly bean shaped two-cylinder Subaru 360 coupe. Banners proclaiming "NEW FOR 1968!" hung from the ceiling of the photo-realistic show-room. Completing the effect was a 1968 reflection of the used car lot opposite the front window with its assortment of trade-in VW Beetles, Renault Dauphines and Chevrolet Corvairs.

Further down the street on the wall of a three-story entertainment mega store, Dorian had captured the Beatles' triumphant arrival at New York's John F. Kennedy Airport in precise life size. Though he had based the mural on a single frame from a black and white newsreel of their first American tour, he had executed it in stunning color, reproducing the gloomy hues of that chilly February day in 1964 so effectively that more than a few passersby shivered—even in the California summer.

Dorian and Griff had to cut short their visit to the zoo where Dorian had covered the exterior wall with a broad panorama depicting the earth's ecosystems. Griff's unfamiliar scent was spooking the zoo's residents who, at the same time, took absolutely no notice of his gargantuan blue tour guide.

The final stop on the tour was the university amphitheater. Dorian had already decked out about two-thirds of the wrap-around wall with depictions of Greco-Roman deities. He knelt down and framed a section of the wall between his claws.

"Diana will go right there." He stood up. "You know what I want to do when this is finished?"

"What?" asked Griff.

"I want to paint you."

Griff smirked. "What color? Pink with purple polka dots?"

"No, not paint *you*, you flea farm! I want to put you on a mural!"

Griff was flattered. "Where?"

"Well, when you called and told me you were coming to California, you mentioned that you read stories to the children at the library in Collinsfort Village. Do you think the townspeople would mind if I immortalized their favorite storyteller on the library wall?"

"I could ask, but even if they say 'no,' you can at least meet the kids and the people in town. Oh, and Bear, too."

"Could I read the kids a story?"

"They'd love that!"

"Great! I'll check my calendar so we can pick a date. Now, let's eat!"

Instead of heading back to the hangar, Dorian led Griff to a small cliff overlooking the sea. The cliff was no higher than a single step for Dorian, but Griff needed a flap of his wings to scale it.

"Wait here," said Dorian, though it was not really necessary; Griff had no intentions of getting his fur and feathers wet.

"Dinner's on me," continued the dragon as he took off his vest and fished a plastic strap from one of the pockets. A waterproof document holder dangled from the strap. Dorian slipped it over his left arm and cinched it midway between his elbow and shoulder.

"What's that?"

"My fishing license." Dorian strode toward the waves. "And our meal ticket. I might look like a big lizard with wings, but the law's the law."

Virtually ignored by the sunbathers and beachcombers, Dorian waded into the water outside the buoys that marked off the swimming area. Beyond the breakers, he launched into a breaststroke and swam until he was the size of a tiny blue lizard against the broad horizon.

Back on the cliff, Griff gazed out over the ocean. An uncomfortable sensation began to creep over him. He looked around and realized he was the target of that suspicious stare reserved for a stranger in town. He tried to melt the icy scrutiny with a warm smile and received a mixture of both smiles and gawks in return.

A pudgy sunbather about eight sizes too large for the skimpy Speedo stretched around his waist lowered his sunglasses, adjusted his straw hat, and resumed reading his Michael Crichton

novel. A little girl waved at Griff, and he waved back. A few souls ventured forward to have their pictures taken with him. One or two who were lucky enough to have brought their copies of *Greatest Chess Matches* to the beach with them nabbed a post-tour autograph.

In about half an hour, Dorian strolled ashore with a large swordfish squirming in one claw and a gray shark writhing about in the other. He held them up. "Guest's choice!" he said.

Though Griff was a graduate of the prestigious Le Cordon Bleu cooking school, he had never filleted a swordfish.

"The shark, please," he said as he stood up. He took the big fish from Dorian and held it firmly. He was about to return to the hangar to clean and cook the shark when Dorian stepped up onto the cliff and sat down. Holding his catch in both claws, Dorian latched his jaws on the fish's sword. With a single sharp twist of his huge head, he snapped off the sword, producing a sound like a muffled firecracker. Griff winced and tried to keep down his lunch.

The sword dangled and jostled in the corner of Dorian's mouth as he crunched into it like a hard breadstick. He swallowed the prickly appetizer and was about to tear into the main course when he noticed Griff had not even started.

"Well, don't just stand there!" he quipped. "Dig in before it gets warm!" With that, he bit into the swordfish's midsection leaving a gaping hole and a perfect dental record.

Griff looked at the shark still struggling to free itself from his claws. He sat down, drew a deep breath and closed his eyes as he whispered, "Bon appétit" to himself. In one swift move, he sank his sharp talons into the shark and bit through its spine. The shark convulsed a few times and went limp. Try as he might, Griff couldn't convince himself that the cold, gelatinous tissue filling his beak was the main ingredient in a warm, fragrant slab of rosemary-grilled shark steak.

"Good, eh?" said Dorian.

Griff stifled a gag and snorted back the tears that had streamed from his eyes into his nostrils. "Marvelous. It's so... fresh!" he wheezed.

Dorian lobbed the picked-clean-to-the-bone skeleton of the swordfish back into the waves. Then he rose and put his vest back on while Griff pitched the remaining three-quarters of the shark into the sea—to the delight of every seagull within ten miles. Dorian finished buttoning his vest and buckled the bottoms of the vest's wing slits. "The sunsets are really spectacular, so I won't mind if you want to stay here while I do some more work on the mural at the university," he said.

Griff pretended to think it over, though in reality he was hoping for a way to evade Dorian and get that awful taste out of his mouth. "Well, I don't come to California very often, so I think I *will* watch the show."

"If I'm asleep when you get back to the hangar, you can open the doors by spelling my name forward and then backward on the security keypad," Dorian explained as he turned back toward the amphitheater.

Griff appeared to be admiring the view, but the moment Dorian was gone, he leaped down from the cliff and headed straight to the pier at the south end of the beach. He waited his turn in line at the hot dog stand.

"Hey, do I know you?" asked the hot dog vendor.

"People say I look like someone on TV," said Griff evasively.

The hot dog vendor thought it over and gave a "makes sense" nod and a shrug. "So, what'll it be?"

Griff loosened the thin, barely visible lanyard that encircled his neck. He swung his wallet around to the front. "A dozen foot-long chili dogs, extra cheese and onions, and a 2-liter Coke."

CHAPTER 10

Autopilot

When Griff awoke he needed a few moments to sort things out. He was buried, as usual, in a pile of straw, but not in the familiar surroundings of the cave he shared with Bear. Instead, he was inside a large, cavernous building. Then he saw Dorian quietly sketching on a large sheet of butcher paper taped to the wall and everything came back to him.

Griff sat up and brushed the straw out of his feathers. In one corner of the hangar, a pair of 120-cup restaurant size coffee urns were chugging away. A box containing a dozen doughnuts sat on one of Dorian's scaffold tables.

Dorian glanced over at Griff. "Coffee's almost ready," he said as he put down his charcoal stick and wiped his claws.

"Thank you," said Griff. "And thank you for the pleasant accommodations." Though Dorian slept directly on the hard concrete floor, he had prepared a corner of the hangar so his guest could get a good night's rest, too. The green "ready to serve" lamp on one of the coffee urns winked on.

Dorian picked up a plastic pail. He had removed the handles from several buckets to make a set of dragon-size coffee cups. "I don't have anything smaller than a gallon bucket."

"Half a bucket will be fine," said Griff as he rose and shook the straw out of his coat. He sauntered over to the box of doughnuts while Dorian drew the coffee. Griff took six doughnuts and nudged the box toward Dorian as his friend set the half-bucket of coffee down on the table.

"They're all yours, Griff," said Dorian. "Remember, I only eat once a day. You, on the other hand, are going to need all that energy to fly home."

Griff nodded. He had alluded to a dragon's dining habits in at least one of Karolyne von Frankenburgh's books, though in that story the beast had devoured a tasty knight in full armor—followed by his horse, saddle, bridle and lance, sighing "Ah, leather and steel... so good for the digestion." Griff tossed a whole glazed doughnut into his beak and followed it with a swig of coffee.

Dorian peeled the butcher paper off the wall and brought it over to where Griff was having breakfast. "Well?"

The paper was covered with several studies of Griff in blissful repose, from a beak-to-tail wide-angle view to a few detailed studies of his claws, feet, tail and face. Near a sketch of Griff peacefully resting his head on his crossed arms Dorian had scribbled, "Aw, ain't he cute?"

"I believe 'dashing' is the word you're looking for," said Griff as he picked up his second doughnut.

Dorian opened the hangar doors and taped the paper to an outside wall. He picked up an aerosol can and commented, "I'm going to lacquer this so you can show it to the people at the library along with my portfolio."

While Griff finished his breakfast, Dorian sprayed a thin layer of fixative over the entire surface of the paper. He stepped back inside and began flipping through the pages of his over-sized reminder calendar.

"I have to go to the dedication and unveiling of the university's mural on the twenty-third of next month, but after that, I'm free. How's the thirtieth?"

"That should be fine. It'll give me a month to tell the people in town about you," said Griff.

Dorian rolled up the charcoal sketch and slipped it into a cylindrical map case. He attached the case to a leather portfolio containing several eleven by fourteen inch photos of his murals.

With the portfolio strapped securely to his back, Griff shared a final farewell hug with Dorian.

"See you in a month," said Dorian. "And remember: An eagle might soar, but a lizard on the ground never crashed into a 747."

Griff laughed, but he wondered what Dorian meant. In flight, Dorian would be an even more spectacular sight than Griff himself.

Griff followed the road down to the beach where he was clear of the airport's flight paths. In five beats of his powerful wings, he was in the air. When he reached cruising altitude, a pair of transparent membranes rose from behind his lower eyelids and covered his eyes. The membranes, which all griffins and dragons had evolved, filtered out the blue of the sky, allowing Griff to see the moon and stars at any time of day.

Locating Orion's Belt, Ursa Major, Ursa Minor and the moon, Griff plotted the first leg of his flight home. When he had his bearings, he put his navigational senses into a mental form of autopilot. Like a freeway motorist whose car is set on cruise control, Griff was free to think about his visit with Dorian and the dragon's forthcoming trip to Collinsfort Village.

Though Griff was nearly fifty years older than Dorian, they had both been born after the era of the griffin-dragon wars.

Griff had heard enough stories of those brutal bygone days to keep Karolyne von Frankenburgh busy for several years at the rate of one new book per year. What appeared to be fanciful fiction was, in fact, mostly based in truth. Griffins were the defenders of humanity in those days, and everything Griff had written about a griffin's combat prowess was true. Though he was modest about it, Griff really was strong enough to break a dragon's neck, and his claws and beak were sharp enough to tear through a dragon's hide.

As humans discovered fire and invented firearms, the griffins had convinced the dragons that even if they joined forces and attacked the human race, they would ultimately be wiped out by humanity's technology and its sheer numbers. A half-dozen renegade dragons and as many griffins jeered such a ridiculous notion and went forth on a mission to cleanse the earth of these pests called Humans. Many thousands of humans were killed in the final battle, but in the end, twelve giant corpses bore silent testimony to mankind's strength in numbers.

The surviving griffins and dragons had made peace with one another and moved into the realms above the clouds, living at altitudes where the air was too thin to sustain human life. Most of them lived unseen, but a few—like Griff and Dorian—had found places where they could become welcome members of society.

Griff had first met Dorian while chronicling a chess tournament in Italy. At the time, Dorian was about the same height as Griff, who was fully grown for a griffin. But at twenty feet, Dorian was still short enough to stand upright inside a cathedral. He had already established himself as a painter of frescoes and murals. However, in time he was forced to limit his artistry to exterior walls as his continuing growth made him much too large to set foot inside most buildings.

As winged giants that still ruled the skies, the two had become fast friends, hunting in the Alps and fishing together across the Mediterranean. When Griff returned to his home in England, he kept in touch with Dorian by letter. But unbeknownst to either of them, the ships carrying their letters were downed in a storm. By the time Griff wrote to the rectory of the cathedral where Dorian had been working, he was informed that Dorian had finished the painting, collected his fee, and gone his way.

Having lost touch with each other, neither one wanted to stay in Europe, so they both made plans to see more of the world. While completing a frieze in a Spanish castle, Dorian heard that an Italian mariner was setting sail under the Spanish flag to find a shorter route to India. The small fleet consisted of three ships. Dorian was able to stand on the deck of the largest without sinking it under his weight, so he answered the call for crewmen. Many years later, Griff followed a ship called the *Mayflower* as it set sail from England. Both friends ended up in the Americas.

The two settled in different parts of what became the United States. Griff found in Bear a kindred spirit and preferred the quiet of the secluded cave, while Dorian eventually settled in the noisy environment of a rented hangar at the California airport.

When the first Karolyne von Frankenburgh books hit the market, Dorian enclosed a picture of himself and some newspaper clippings about his paintings in a fan letter to the author. "If you're who I think you are, you'll know who I am," was all he wrote. Griff knew immediately who it was, though the dragon in the photo was twice as large as Griff remembered, judging from the people and buildings in the picture.

Griff's writing and Dorian's mural painting kept them too busy to find the time for a visit. But eventually, when Griff had fulfilled his contractual obligations to the publishers of the Karolyne von Frankenburgh books, he was able to write his own book on chess. The book tour that followed was a perfect opportunity to see Dorian again, and by lucky coincidence, Dorian had caught up on his own commitments. In a month, the magnificent peacock-blue dragon would be dancing across the skies above Collinsfort Village, bathing the town in rainbow hues. Griff couldn't wait to get home so he could tell everyone the news.

As dusk approached, Griff yawned and took another reading from the stars to verify his position. He was nearly over Salt Lake City, Utah. Somewhere below, in the grand ballroom of the city's most historic hotel, a fresh pile of straw and a DO NOT DISTURB sign were waiting for him. There were no books to sign tonight, just peaceful rest. He ceased flapping his wings and glided toward the winking lights of the city.

Dragon, Fly!

A Grand Entrance... Sort Of

Griff returned home to Collinsfort Village and spent the month preparing the town for Dorian's visit. He presented Dorian's offer of a library mural to a special session of the city council, highlighting the proposal with Dorian's portfolio and the charcoal studies. The vote was a unanimous Yea. Griff called Dorian with the good news, and Dorian soon had several gallons of titanium white paint shipped to the library with instructions to apply it to the wall on which they wanted the mural.

For his Saturday story times, Griff read all the stories he could find about friendly dragons. The children were perfectly comfortable with Griff, but he had no way to predict their reaction to a dragon twice his size. By the final week before Dorian's visit, however, Griff was certain the children would run eagerly to meet the huge dragon, even if he was sixty feet tall.

On Saturday, half the town seemed to be making its way up Griff and Bear's mountain. Griff had told everyone about the glorious spectacle they'd miss if they did not see Dorian in flight. He directed both motorized and foot traffic. Meanwhile Bear, in a snappy three-piece tailored suit, conferred with the newspaper reporters and TV news crews who had joined the growing throng. A large circular landing pad had been roped off, and it was soon surrounded with eager onlookers. By mid-morning, every eye was trained on the sky.

"Is that him? Is that him?" yelled one of the children, pointing and jumping up and down.

"No, Kyle, that's a bald eagle," said Griff.

"I see him!" shouted another.

"No, Cindy, that's a helicopter."

"Why didn't they hire Dorian to paint the ceiling of the Sistine Chapel?"

Griff chuckled. "Ask him when he gets here, Dennis."

A few minutes later, something big with wings appeared over the distant horizon. Its shadow swept over the town and enveloped the mountain in darkness.

"It's only a Boeing 747 on final approach to Denver," said Griff before any of the children could speak.

"Actually, that's a new Airbus A380—the biggest passenger jet in the world," said a voice from above and behind the crowd. "And I should know. I live at an airport."

"Great hounds of Zeus!" yelled Griff as he leaped into the air in shock and recognition. He had turned halfway around by the time he came back to earth. Now everyone else turned and looked up at the source of the voice.

Standing at the edge of the crowd in all his peacock blue glory was Dorian. In each claw was a large footlocker, and across his back, strapped between his wings, was a disassembled scaffold. He dropped to his knees, set down his load, and threw open his arms, visibly pleased that he had surprised everyone, including the sharp-eared Griff.

"Here there be Dorian!" cried Griff. They shared a friendly hug, and when they parted Dorian stayed on his knees while Griff stood at his side.

"Well, let's get acquainted, everyone! My name's Dorian di Drago, but you can just call me Dorian. 'Mister di Drago' was my daddy's name."

A woman in a gray business suit stepped forward from the crowd and presented her right hand to the towering blue visitor. "Justine Pearson, mayor of Collinsfort Village," she said. "Welcome to our town, Dorian!"

"The pleasure is mine, Madame Mayor," said Dorian as he shook her hand. The press photographers and news crews surged forward to capture the moment. Three women and four men, also dressed in business attire, gathered around Mayor Pearson.

"This is our city council. They voted unanimously to accept your offer of a mural," said the mayor.

"Always glad to meet people with good taste!" said Dorian.

One by one, the city council members introduced themselves and shook hands with Dorian. Griff could not be sure, but as each council member passed by and glanced at him, they seemed to be disappointed.

The same was true of everyone else who stepped forward to meet Dorian. They were impressed with his gentle nature and huge size, but they gave Griff a look that said, "Big letdown."

When the greetings were done, Dorian stood up. "Now, if you don't mind, I'd like to see my home away from home for the next month," he said as he picked up his footlockers.

"Right this way!" said Griff. He led Dorian to the cliff overlooking the town.

Dorian stepped to the edge and took in the view. "Ah, *there's* the airport!"

"Yes, your domicile awaits! Follow me!" said Griff, launching himself over the cliff.

"I'll catch up to you!" yelled Dorian. He turned and started walking along the road that zigzagged down the side of the mountain. An impromptu parade of townspeople fell in line behind him. Griff flew on ahead and waited by the hangar doors for Dorian and his spontaneous entourage.

"No, Dennis, Michelangelo undercut my bid and the rest is history," said Dorian as they arrived.

"Were you bummed out about it?" asked Dennis.

Dorian assumed an Italian accent. "Eh, whaddya gonna do? If the guy wants to spend four years on his back six inches from the ceiling, who am I to stop him? Back then, I would have needed a scaffold myself, and there wasn't enough lumber in all of Italy to build one that would hold me."

"Can I watch you work on the mural for a school project?"

"Hey, knock yourself out! The more, the merrier. Just stay clear of all moving parts of the artist," said Dorian. "I was painting an ad for a steakhouse on the side of a barn, and I took out six Black Angus steers with my tail."

"Was the cattle rancher mad at you?"

"Sure, but we worked things out. I knocked half off my fee, and he let me have the steers for dinner."

"That sounds about right," said Dennis as he turned to leave with the rest of the townsfolk.

"Smart kid," said Dorian.

"Trust me, you wouldn't have said that about him just two years ago," said Griff as he turned his attention to the chain and pulley that opened the hangar doors. "Well, it's not as fancy as home, but I hope it'll do." He stooped down inside the door and switched on the lights.

Dorian stepped inside and walked around. A big screen

TV occupied one corner of the hangar and a speakerphone was mounted thirty feet above the floor on one of the walls. Along another wall, several utility shelves had been erected and stocked with the paints Dorian had ordered from a home improvement center in Fort Collins. "It's perfect!" he declared. He set down the footlockers and the scaffold.

"Need any help unpacking?" asked Griff.

"No, but we'll have to go to town on Monday so I can get a Colorado fish and game license. They said I could use my California license over the weekend."

"Use it for what?"

"Dinner. There are plenty of deer, elk and moose up in them thar hills," said Dorian with a big sharp-toothed grin.

Griff reacted with an uneasy grimace.

"Oh, don't give me that look," replied Dorian. "You used to pick off a deer on the run as easily as an eagle snagging a rabbit."

"That was before I became a grand master of the culinary arts," said Griff.

Dorian pretended to be impressed. "Ooh! Well, don't worry about it. I'll be hunting so deep in the woods, no one will ever know."

"Thank you. But just to be sure, do me a favor."

"What's that?"

"Don't let any of the kids watch," said Griff.

CHAPTER 12

Confession

Carl Lumbly, the local Fish and Game officer, stepped out onto the sidewalk where Dorian and Griff were waiting.

"Sorry this took so long," he said. "They didn't have the proper forms in Fort Collins, so I had to wait for the office in Denver to fax them over. Now, which of you is applying for the Special Non-Resident Colorado Fish and Game License?"

Griff crossed his arms, looked straight at Carl, and said nothing. He had lived on the mountain near Collinsfort Village since before Carl was born. Carl's son Chris was a regular at his story times.

Carl sighed in exasperation and looked up at Dorian. With his pen poised on the first line of the form and resignation obvious in his voice he said, "Full legal name, last name first."

"Di Drago, Dorian Damiano."

"Residence address?"

"Twenty-three thirty, Airport Service Road, Santa Barbara, California, ZIP code nine-three-one-zero-five."

"Citizenship?"

"United States."

"Country of birth?"

"Tuscany, uh, Italy."

"Date of birth?"

"Julian or Gregorian calendar?"

"Never mind. You're over a hundred years old, aren't you?"

Dorian nodded, and Carl marked the space "N/A." "Trophy or food license?"

"I'm not into animal cruelty."

Carl glared up at Dorian. "I'll take that to mean food."

Dorian nodded again.

"Everyone's a #!@ *$&^#@! bunny-hugger now days," Carl muttered. He sized up Dorian and flipped through a series of charts on his clipboard. "Mr. di Drago," he declared in a very official voice, "your daily limit is three deer, or two elk, or two moose—or the equivalent thereof. If you exceed your limit, you will be subject to revocation of your license and/or arrest. In the interest of conservation, please refrain from taking juveniles, pregnant females or females of offspring-bearing age. Please display your license at all times while hunting, and observe all safe hunting practices. The processing fee is fifteen dollars."

Dorian reached into a pocket in his vest and took out his wallet. He removed a twenty-dollar bill and handed it down to Carl.

"Give me a couple of minutes to punch this into the computer, and I'll be right back with your license and change," Carl said as he went inside.

Dorian looked toward the mountains; he licked his chops and patted his belly. "Mmm, mighty fine dining up there!"

"Knock it off," snapped Griff.

Dorian dropped his claw to his side. "Party pooper." He peered over the two-story government building at the parking lot beyond.

"So, which pickup does Carl drive?"

"The red Ford with *two* gun racks," said Griff.

Dorian gave an "I thought so" nod.

"And a golden retriever?"

"Carl's a black Lab kind of guy."

With the hunting license finally in hand, the next stop was the library. A large sign had been erected near the white, newly painted wall. "Collinsfort Village Arts Council proudly presents DORIAN di DRAGO, Muralist at Large," it proclaimed. Dorian's concept drawing of the mural took up the rest of the sign. It depicted the mural as a life-size cutaway view of the library—like a giant doll's house with the windows suspended in space. In the mural, Griff was reading aloud to an audience of Collinsfort Village children and several familiar storybook characters.

Under Dennis' constant observation, Dorian began sketching the mural directly on the wall.

"Aren't you going to use a cartoon?" asked Dennis. He was referring to a life-size sketch coated on the back with charcoal. The artist would rub the outlines of the sketch with a wooden dowel to transfer a carbon copy onto the wall.

"Not for the background," answered Dorian. "I'll use cartoons for the live models. Do you want to be in the mural?"

"Yeah!" said Dennis.

"Bring your favorite book with you tomorrow, and I'll make a cartoon of you."

As he outlined the library's interior on the wall, Dorian

took several sightings through each window, compensating for his limited view of the inside.

Each morning for the next few days, Griff flew down from the mountain to Dorian's hangar where he joined the dragon on his daily stroll to the library. Griff spent the day reading. Dorian spent the day drawing. Dennis took notes and made sketches in a sketch pad. In the evening, Dennis biked home while Griff flew back to the cave and Dorian hiked into the higher elevations of the Rocky Mountains to catch and eat his dinner.

Maybe Griff was only imagining it, but Dorian seemed to be spending too much time on the ground. Even back when he and Dorian were still the same height, Griff had been forced to admit that Dorian was more impressive in flight than Griff himself. At his present size, Dorian would be even more magnificent in the air. Dragons were, after all, aerial hunters, swooping down from above and snatching their prey on the run. Yet Griff could not recall seeing Dorian in the sky over the alpine forests. Instead, Dorian ambled into the woods as if he were merely sightseeing and emerged an hour or so later, giving absolutely no clue that he had reduced the antelope population by one or two adults.

On Saturday, Griff came home with the groceries and found Bear and Dennis perched in Bear's astronomy loft. Bear peered through his telescope toward the mountains while Dennis held a pair of binoculars to his eyes.

"A little early for stargazing, isn't it?" said Griff.

"Shhhh, be vewwy, vewwy quiet," said Dennis mimicking a well-known cartoon character.

Bear continued in the same voice. "We're hunting the ewusive, fwightwess, peacock-bwoo, wainbow-winged pawadox."

Griff sighed and looked up at the mountains. "I've been

meaning to talk to him about that," he said as his ears picked up the spirited protests of a bull elk becoming Dorian's dinner. The sound was too faint for Dennis or Bear to hear.

"When?" demanded Bear. "You know, the buzz in town is *not* that he's here to paint a mural. All anyone's talking about is what a big letdown he is. These people want to see him fly, and if he doesn't start logging some serious air time, they're going to run him out of town before the mural's half finished."

Griff turned toward Dennis hoping to find an ally, but he came up empty.

"My school project is about how an artist paints a mural *and* how a dragon flies. I'll be lucky if I get a C-minus," Dennis lamented.

Bear cradled Dennis' face in his paws. Dennis played along, looking at Griff with big pleading eyes while Bear spoke in a melodramatic tone. "Look at this face. How can you let down a kid like this, Griff? He looks up to you. Actually, everyone in town looks up to you. They can't help it, but you know what I mean. Do you really want this innocent child to show his mom and dad a C-minus?"

Griff looked into their dramatic pleading eyes and said simply, "Dinner will be ready in an hour and a half; I presume Dennis is staying?"

Bear and Dennis nodded in unison.

As Griff shredded a block of cheddar for a batch of potatoes au gratin, he devised a plan. Dorian was to be next Saturday's special guest reader at the library. Since he was too big to fit inside, his story time would be held in the civic center amphitheater, giving him a chance to study the children's facial expressions for their depiction in the mural.

Griff waited until Friday to set his trap for the giant, blue earthbound dragon. At the end of the day, Dorian tapped on the library window as a signal to Griff that he was finished. Griff stood up and stretched, set his books on a return cart and sauntered outside where Dorian was wiping the charcoal dust from his claws with a bed sheet.

"Can you stop by the cave tomorrow morning before story time?" asked Griff. "I have something to show you that's too big to bring to the library."

"What time?" asked Dorian as he folded the sheet and dropped it into one of his footlockers. He closed the lid and clicked a padlock in place before tucking the lockers inside the library's service entrance.

"Come by at eight," said Griff, and he took off into the air.

"I'll be there," Dorian called.

The next day, true to his word, Dorian arrived at the cave a few minutes before eight in the morning.

"Hi, Mister Bear! Can Griff come out to play?" he said as Bear opened the front door.

Bear laughed. "Your little friend's here, Griff!" he shouted over his shoulder. Griff stepped outside.

"Okay, where's this 'thing' you want to show me?" said Dorian.

"Right over here."

Griff led Dorian to the edge of the cliff. Dorian peered off into the distance.

"Where?"

Griff pointed a single talon at the library. "Right there."

"The library?"

"Yes. Let's go to the library, Dorian."

Dorian began to wonder what Griff was up to. "Okay, but story time is still two hours away," he said nonchalantly. He turned toward the dirt road.

"*Not that way,*" barked Griff in a voice better suited to a drill sergeant.

Dorian froze in mid-stride. He exhaled a couple of nervous breaths and tried to keep the conversation on the light side. "There's another way?" he said with a panicky laugh.

"You *know* there is," said Griff in the same commanding tone. "The same way *I* get there."

Dorian turned and slowly walked back to the cliff. He stood at the edge and looked out over the town for what seemed like an eternity.

Griff waited patiently.

Finally, Dorian squatted down, and for a moment, Griff thought the dragon was preparing to launch himself into the air. Instead, Dorian sat down on the ground with his legs dangling over the edge of the cliff. Even seated, he was still taller than Griff, but surrounded by the immenseness of the aerial domain he had once ruled, he looked small, helpless and defeated.

Griff sat down next to him but said nothing.

Eventually, Dorian broke the silence. "Is it really that obvious, Griff?"

"Like a moustache on the *Mona Lisa.*"

Dorian sighed heavily. "I haven't flown in almost a hundred years," he said, still staring into the empty air above the town. He turned his head to follow the flight of a passing bald eagle. "There's a beautiful little island about a hundred miles off the coast of Santa Barbara. I used to fish from there, but now I can only fish as far as I can swim. It's been ages since I've caught a great white shark or a giant squid for dinner. If I tried to fly home right now, I probably wouldn't even recognize Santa Barbara from the air."

He drew up the courage to go on and looked down at Griff. His green reptilian eyes usually sparkled like polished jade spheres, but now they were clouded with more than a half century of pain, suffering and guilt.

"I'm about to tell you something I've never told anyone. I changed aviation history, Griff. If the rest of the world ever found out, they'd want me dead."

"What happened, Dorian?"

Dorian reached into a vest pocket and took out a leather portfolio. It opened to reveal a pair of eight by ten photos. He stared at the pictures for a few moments before handing the portfolio to Griff.

"Recognize her?"

The woman wore a blouse, a skirt and a loosely tied silk scarf in the posed studio photo on the left. In the other, she was dressed for a day of flying with a pair of aviator goggles perched atop her leather helmet.

"This is Amelia Earhart," said Griff.

Dorian closed his eyes. A tear trickled from behind his eyelid as he nodded.

"I think I killed her, Griff."

CHAPTER 13

Story Time, Times Two

Dorian looked out over the town again. He appeared to be gathering his thoughts. Finally, he rose to his feet.

Griff could see that Dorian was ready to talk. He stood up as well. "Nice day for a walk," he said. "I think I'll take the scenic route to the library, too." He handed back the portfolio, and the two friends set off down the road. As they rounded the first bend with the cave no longer in sight, Dorian launched into his story.

"It was 1937 and the Fourth of July weekend was coming up. I was flying home from that island I told you about with a half-dozen of the biggest deep-sea octopuses you ever saw, when one of those Pacific summer storms came out of nowhere. The wind blew me off course and slammed me around so much that I lost my bearings. I thought I was climbing toward the clouds, but I was really heading straight for the water. If I hadn't pulled up just in time I would have drowned, Griff."

Griff knew what Dorian meant. A griffin could take off from land or sea, but a dragon in the water with no solid land within swimming distance was doomed.

"I turned around so sharply that I thought my canards were going to snap right off. I dropped my catch and tried to climb above the storm to get my bearings again. When I finally broke through the clouds, I was on a collision course with a small airplane. I yelled for the pilot to pull up, but I'm sure I was drowned out by the engine noise and the storm. When it looked like we were going to crash, I turned a full back flip. I heard the plane's engine throttling all the way up." Dorian paused and swung his tail within reach of his right claw. He held the end at Griff's eye level. "You see that scar?"

Griff nodded as he made out the three-foot-long fissure in Dorian's hide and the misaligned scales on either side.

"That's where the propeller hit me just as I was ditching back into the storm. After another few minutes of being chucked around like a dishrag in a washing machine, I climbed above the clouds again, but the plane was nowhere in sight. I was tired and hungry, and by the stars, I was about two hundred miles northwest of Santa Barbara. I headed home above the clouds, and the storm fizzled out by the time I got back to the coast. When I finally landed, I was really famished, so I rested a while, and after that, I went for a swim, caught a shark, and had dinner on the beach.

"On the way home, I kept passing mobs of people huddled around any radio they could find. Outside a furniture store where they sold those big old Philco radios, they had four of them lined up on the sidewalk with the volume turned all the way up. The sidewalk was jammed with people listening.

"Paolo, the guy who mixed paint for me at the hardware store, was at the back of the crowd, so I asked him what had happened. He said Amelia Earhart's plane was missing. Went down somewhere over the Pacific, they thought.

"It was like someone had dropped a whole planet on me, Griff. That plane was hers. I'm sure it was. I felt so sick that I slunk into my hangar, shut the doors and windows, and didn't come out for three days. After that, I never flew again. I didn't want to risk taking another life."

Dorian sniffled loudly as his eyes misted up again.

"Are you going to be okay?" Griff asked. "Do you want me to read to the children?"

"No, I'll be fine. This always happens when I think about it."

"And how often *do* you think about it?"

"Only every night," said Dorian in a quivery voice, tears pouring from his eyes, "but usually, when I'm alone so no one will see me like this." He made no effort to conceal his tears.

"Your wings look as if you never gave up flying, and I *know* a dragon's flight vest when I see one," said Griff, noting the fitness of Dorian's wings and the heavy-duty pocket buckles and roomy wing slits of his vest.

"I exercise my wings every night and tell myself that tomorrow I'll fly again, but I never do. A thousand times a day, I think about jumping into the sky and flying until I can't fly any farther, and a thousand times a day, I think of what I did to Amelia. It could happen all over again, only much worse. The skies are a lot more crowded these days.

"If I had the guts, I'd ask you to rip my wings off at the roots so I wouldn't have a reason to even *think* about flying, but I'm not brave enough. Griff, I've lived on the ground for so long, I'm ready to spend the rest of my life here."

"But look at what it's doing to you," said Griff. "You look like a flock of griffins used you for a rugby ball, and that's just from telling me about it."

"Oh, that's easy to fix," said Dorian. He took a deep breath and exhaled with a violent shudder. His eyes began to clear and his jovial, carefree façade returned to shield him from the past. "There! Good as new! See?" he said with a big toothy smile.

Griff was startled by the maneuver but duly impressed. He paused to make some quick calculations. "You telephoned me before you left Santa Barbara," he said, "and you arrived in Collinsfort Village four days later. An eagle would have to fly at least twelve hours a day to cover that same distance. How did you do it on foot?"

"Road running," said Dorian with a grin.

Griff arched his eyebrows into a look of doubt. "You mean like that silly bird in the Warner Brothers cartoons?"

Dorian nodded, still grinning.

Griff came to a halt and crossed his arms. "Show me," he demanded.

Dorian shrugged and trotted about a quarter-mile down the road. He turned, leaned forward nearly to the ground with his tail long and straight behind him and spread his wings slightly. Suddenly, he was off. His feet were a spinning blur as he barreled down the road at the speed of a sports car, leaving a cloud of dust but hardly a trace of a footprint in the dirt. He shot past the stunned griffin and stopped about a half-mile beyond. As he walked back to where Griff stood, he folded his wings and resumed his normal upright stance.

Griff stared up at him with a vacant look.

"What's wrong?" asked Dorian.

"I'm going to have nightmares for weeks about a gigantic coyote chasing you with a knife and fork," said Griff. He closed his eyes and shook his head, hoping to dislodge the image before it settled in his unconscious mind.

They resumed their walk to the library in silence. After several moments, Griff spoke up.

"How on earth did you do that without causing a pileup on the highway?"

"Back roads at night."

"Of course," said Griff in a how-stupid-of-me… everyone-knows-that tone.

Griff and Dorian arrived at the library with an hour to spare before story time. While Dorian touched up a few details on the mural, Griff pulled open the library's tall double doors. A pedestal sign had been placed on the atrium steps where Griff usually sat to read to the children. "Special Guest Reader," it announced. "Muralist DORIAN di DRAGO, in the Civic Center Amphitheater, 10:00 a.m."

Griff approached the head librarian's desk with a wave. "Hi, Evelyn. Have you got the books for our guest reader?"

"Right here!" She patted the handle of a cart holding several two-foot by three-foot, oversized read-aloud books. Griff looked over Dorian's selection of titles, which included *Where the Wild Things Are*, *The Reluctant Dragon*, *Fantastic Mr. Fox* and Karolyne von Frankenburgh's only picture book, *The Hopscotch Dragon*.

"The children will love these!" Griff proclaimed. He carried the books to the amphitheater and laid them on the stage. He then opened the scenery shed and dragged out a twenty-foot-tall plywood cutout of a sprawling castle that had been constructed for the Village Minstrels' recent production of *Camelot*. After placing the castle center stage, he sat down at the edge of the stage and waited for the children to arrive.

Dorian wanted to make an impressive entrance, so when he was finished working on the mural he put away his trunks and crouched down behind the plywood castle.

Griff picked up *The Hopscotch Dragon* and pretended to read

with rapt attention while the children filed into the amphitheater. As the last of the children took their seats, he looked up from the book.

"Once upon a time," he began, "there was a dragon named Dorian. He was as blue as a peacock, with eyes the color of jade and wings that turned sunlight into rainbows. He could paint a mural as beautifully as any of the masters. And Dorian was very… *very*… VERY… big."

Dorian reached up and draped a claw over the castle roof while wrapping the other around one of the towers. The children snickered and giggled as he slowly rose to his feet, dwarfing the castle. He strode around to the front of the stage as Griff stood up and led the children in a round of applause.

Dorian took a bow. "Good morning, Collinsfort Village!" he boomed.

"Good morning, Dorian!" the children shouted in unison.

Dorian sat down with his feet resting in the orchestra pit. "Thank you, Mr. Griffin!" he said as Griff handed him the jumbo-sized copy of *The Hopscotch Dragon*. The book nestled into Dorian's immense claws like a mass-market paperback. "So, who wants to hear a story?"

The young audience erupted into shouts of "I do!" and "We do!" and "Me! Me!" while Dorian took a pair of tiny reading glasses from his vest pocket. He rested the glasses on his snout and opened *The Hopscotch Dragon* to the first page.

When Dorian was well into the story, Griff quietly slipped back inside the library. He searched in vain for the microfilm section and then asked the assistant librarian for help.

"We don't have microfilm anymore, Griff," said Larry. "We have DNA."

"Well, neither of us would be here if we didn't," replied Griff, "but how is that going to help me find some old newspapers?"

Larry grinned. "Come this way."

He led Griff to the corner of the library that had once been occupied by the microfilm readers.

"DNA is the Digital Newspaper Archive," said Larry. He stopped near a cluster of computers equipped with 21-inch flat-panel monitors. "You can pull up just about any newspaper published anywhere in the world, from last month all the way back to Gutenberg's first edition."

Griff shot Larry a look of doubt.

"Well, okay, maybe not *that* far back. Follow the instructions on the screen, and if you want any printouts, you can buy a cash card from the machine near the copiers."

Griff sat on the floor in front of the nearest computer. He took his reading glasses and unsharpened pencils from his wallet and typed in "Amelia Earhart, 1937, Santa Barbara, California."

Griff limited his search to the newspapers Dorian might have read right after his near collision with the plane. The computer retrieved the front page of the July 3, 1937, Santa Barbara *Coastal Dispatch* and the Santa Barbara *Sun.* Both carried the same wire service story of Amelia Earhart's disappearance, and both were illustrated with nearly identical photos.

Griff looked at the story in the *Dispatch* first. Details were sketchy since the story was made up of bits and pieces of preliminary information. He read all the way through the article then returned to the Santa Barbara *Sun's* version to see if it had any more information. He reached the end of the text on the front page and used the mouse to click "cont. on page A-8."

On the jump page, the *Sun* had printed more photos of Amelia Earhart than the *Dispatch*.

While Griff scrolled down through the story, Dennis approached the table opposite where Griff was seated. Dennis had been using the DNA to find articles about Dorian's mural painting. He carried two large coffee table books—about Michelangelo and Leonardo da Vinci—and when he plopped them down on his table, their weight jostled both tables. Griff's computer mouse lurched, and he scrolled past the end of the story. He snorted in exasperation.

"Sorry," said Dennis as he sat down.

Griff was about to scroll back to the Earhart story when another headline caught his eye. It was over a short three-paragraph article near the bottom of the page.

AIRMAIL PILOT SAYS "IT WAS BIGGER THAN AN AIRPLANE"

San Francisco, July 3 (AP) -- Airmail pilot Gordon Mitchell of Alameda had to be helped from his plane after arriving yesterday at the U.S. Post Office depot of the San Francisco Airport. The pilot, who holds a perfect safety and punctuality record on the Honolulu-to-San Francisco route, was babbling incoherently about nearly colliding with something that he claimed was "a [heck] of a lot bigger than an airplane."

Mitchell went on to say that the flying object did not produce any engine noise, nor did it bear markings identifying it as any type of civilian or military aircraft. He said the object emerged from a cloud bank above a Pacific storm and quickly dived back into the clouds while Mitchell attempted to pull up to avoid colliding with it.

Mitchell was admitted to the psychiatric ward at San Francisco General Hospital for observation and was released after testing failed to reveal any evidence of mental illness or drunkenness.

The story was repeated in the *Dispatch*, but not on the same page as the Earhart coverage.

Griff started a new search, this time zeroing in on San Francisco newspapers from the same date.

The San Francisco *Journal* carried the story with a portrait of Gordon Mitchell in uniform. The *Bay Herald's* version was illustrated with a photo of Mitchell standing beside his plane, but the picture was so tightly cropped that little of the plane was visible.

Griff looked over his monitor at Dennis. "Are you terribly busy with your school project, Dennis?"

Dennis finished copying a few notes from the Michelangelo book. "No, not really. I could use a break." He leaned back in his chair and stretched.

"Would you like to do a little detective work with me?"

"Yeah!" said Dennis. He parked a couple of pens behind his ear. "What's the case, Chief?"

"What do you know about a woman named Amelia Earhart?"

"I know she tried to fly around the world, but she never made it."

"Well, we're going to find out what happened on the day her plane disappeared." Griff clicked his mouse on the File menu. He selected the "Lock computer for up to three minutes" option. When he was prompted for a password to unlock the computer, he entered the word "Earhart."

"Sorry, password must be at least eight letters, numbers and/or symbols in length," the computer informed him.

Griff typed "Amelia-Earhart." The computer accepted the password, and a picture of a large padlock and a clock ticking off three minutes appeared on the screen.

"Wait here and make sure no one touches this computer," said Griff as he stood up and swung his wallet around to the front of his neck. He strode over to the cash card vending machines and came back with a pair of the cards. He handed one to Dennis.

"Go to one of the Internet computers and look up everything you can about Amelia Earhart. We'll need maps, flight plans, pilot's logs... anything you can find about her last flight. We'll also need a Mercator projection map of the entire world. Print it all out and meet me on the atrium steps in a half-hour."

"Right, Chief!" Dennis bolted out of his chair toward an unoccupied Internet computer.

"Oh, and Dennis?" said Griff.

Dennis stopped and turned. "Yeah, Chief?"

"Don't call me 'Chief.' We're private investigators, not the police."

"Okay, Boss!" Dennis took off once more.

Griff mouthed the word, "Boss" and shook his head. He could live with that.

Dennis and Griff attacked their research with the determination of a wolverine trying to unearth a stubborn hare. Every few minutes, the quiet of the library was interrupted with a gentle "A-ha!" from Griff or Dennis' victory cry of "All right!"

Thirty minutes later, they sat down on the top atrium step to compare notes.

"I'll need the world map first, Dennis," said Griff.

Dennis pulled the map from his sheaf of printouts. "Here you go, Boss."

Griff laid the map on the floor and took a pair of colored markers from his wallet. With a blue marker, he drew a pair of arcing lines connecting California with Hawaii.

"Should I pack for a trip to Hawaii, Boss?" asked Dennis.

"No, Dennis. These are the old airmail routes between San Francisco and Honolulu."

"What does it have to do with Amelia Earhart?"

"I'm not sure yet. Do you have a map of her final flight?"

"Way ahead of you," said Dennis. He already had the map at the top of his stack.

Griff began plotting Earhart's route on the world map with a red marker, and right away he saw that something was wrong. Amelia and her navigator took off from Oakland, California and headed eastward through Tucson, New Orleans and Miami. From there, they followed the Atlantic coast of South America before continuing across Africa and Asia. Beyond New Guinea, and somewhere over Howland Island in the Pacific Ocean, the plane vanished. "This doesn't make any sense at all," Griff murmured. "She's obviously riding the trade winds, but she's going the wrong way."

"You mean she might have made it if she had been flying east to west?" asked Dennis.

Griff barely heard the question. He began thinking out loud while picking out points on the map with his talon. "Amelia is there, the airmail routes are over here, and this is Santa Barbara, so there's no way Dorian could have crossed paths with Amelia Earhart's plane."

"What?" cried Dennis, astonished.

Griff snapped out of his half-trance with a jolt. He quickly gathered together his printouts and maps. "Nothing, Dennis!"

Griff stood up and took off toward the library door. "Auditory hallucination! Your ears are playing tricks on you."

Dennis scooped up his own materials and scrambled to his feet. "Tell me what you meant!" he demanded as he ran after Griff.

Griff arrived at the door well ahead of Dennis, but he had to slow down as he stooped under the doorway. It was just enough time for Dennis to slalom through his legs and out onto the walkway.

Dennis planted himself directly in Griff's path. "You're not getting past me until you come clean, Griff!"

Griff leaned forward until his beak was inches from Dennis' face. He curled his claws into menacing hooks as if he were about to attack small prey. "Get out of my way, or I'll turn you into a pile of fresh-ground Dennis-burger," said Griff in a voice that made the pavement tremble.

"You think you can scare me? I've already been mauled to death by Bear and lived to tell about it."

Griff straightened up, crossed his arms, and looked down his beak at Dennis. "Come to think of it, Dennis, you're not worth getting into trouble with the law. All I have to do is walk around you."

"I wouldn't do that if I were you, Griff."

"And why not?"

"There's steer manure on the grass. You want to track bull poop all over Bear's favorite Persian rug?"

"You know, Dennis, arguing with you is the biggest waste of breath in the world." Griff turned around and spread his wings.

"Go ahead, you big chicken! Fly away and hide in your cave! Tell Bear that big, mean Dennis is after you! I can't believe I did all that work for you, and you won't even tell me what we were really looking for! It has something to do with Dorian, doesn't it?"

Griff sighed and folded his wings. He turned to face Dennis. "What is it about keeping secrets that brings out the worst in you and me?"

Dennis' scowl faded into a grin, which led to a snicker followed by full-blown laughter. By the time they made it back to the atrium steps, Griff was laughing, too. Through the window, they watched a five-year-old St. George pretending to slay a mural-painting Reluctant Dragon on the amphitheater stage.

"Wait until Dorian finishes reading to the children, then meet me at the riding academy," said Griff. "I may be strong enough to lift a dragon off the ground, but I don't know if I can make him fly all by myself."

CHAPTER 14

The Connection

On Monday, work on the mural resumed. Dorian lay on his side with his neck twisted to keep his eyes parallel to the ground. Using a human-sized paintbrush, he added the final details to Griff's likeness. Griff's audience would be painted in over the next several days.

Dennis documented every step in his notebook and sketch pad. He had to fight the temptation to stare at Dorian while contemplating what Griff had told him.

Dorian pulled himself up from the ground and tapped on the library window to get Griff's attention. When Griff looked up from his reading, Dorian grinned and gave him an OK hand signal. Griff nodded back, set his book aside and joined Dorian outside.

"So, what do you think?" asked Dorian. He gestured toward the image of Griff on the library wall.

Though Griff had seen his reflection many times, in all his many centuries he had never seen himself drawn actual size. He was overwhelmed by his own immenseness.

"You've turned me into a monster!" he cried. "That brute could pick up a cow in each claw and still bite off a hippo's head with his beak! I can't possibly be *that* huge!"

"Happens every time," said Dorian with a sigh. He reached

into one of his trunks and took out a retractable metal measuring tape. "Sit down," he said as he dropped to one knee and extended the tape.

Griff dutifully sat as Dorian measured him from the tips of his ears to his rump and locked the tape in place.

"See for yourself," Dorian said, handing Griff the tape.

Griff double-checked his sitting height. Then he stood up and held the tape near his painted likeness, taking care not to touch the wet paint.

"Mister Pearson," said Dorian. "Please explain to the subject what he has just experienced."

Dennis looked up from his sketch pad.

"It is a little-known fact," he recited, "that a reflection viewed at a distance where one can see one's full height is actually only half life-size, giving the illusion that the life-size image is much larger."

"Perfecto!" said Dorian.

"Yes, I see," said Griff as he reeled in the tape. He handed it back to Dorian and studied the image. "I suppose the effect *is* more stately than frightening," he conceded. "I never knew there was so much of me to love."

Dorian laughed and dropped the measuring tape into his trunk. He sat down as Dennis brought over his latest batch of sketches. Dorian studied each sketch, pausing here and there to examine the details and then declared, "These are amazing, Dennis. How long have you been drawing?"

Dennis took a piece of paper from his folio and handed it to Dorian. "My mom says I drew this when I was little, but I don't even remember it."

"A self-portrait. Impressive."

"No, that's my brother Kevin. He was five, and I was

three. I guess I could always draw, but I never thought it was anything special. When I was seven, an art teacher at school called me a prodigy, but everyone else called me 'The Human Camera' or 'Mr. Polaroid,' so I stopped drawing pictures of the other kids in class."

"Those are compliments, Dennis," said Dorian. "When I get back to the hangar, I'm going to call the Arts Council. They really should see these. Mind if I take a few with me?"

"Yeah, sure, go ahead," said Dennis.

Dorian picked out four sketches and the picture of Kevin.

As Dennis pedaled away on his bicycle, Dorian leaned back and massaged his neck. With more than seven times as many vertebrae as a human, a dragon's swan-like neck was very prone to developing kinks during times of intense concentration.

"If you no longer require my services," Griff interrupted, "I'll return to *my* work-in-progress."

"What's that?" asked Dorian. He turned his head a full two hundred and seventy degrees, causing the joints in his neck to emit a series of cracking and popping sounds.

"I'm writing an article that I want to submit to *Smithsonian* magazine. It's about airmail pilots and the early days of the airmail service," he said. He studied Dorian's face for any hint of an unusual reaction.

"Sounds interesting," said Dorian smoothly. "I'd like to have a look at it when it's finished." He unwound his neck with a sigh of contentment.

"Gladly," said Griff as he took to the air, though to himself he muttered, "I'll *bet* you would."

Griff had spent all of Sunday at his writing table working on "his project" with a speakerphone and several pages of telephone listings. Bear had compiled the listings from Internet phone directories and his phone company contacts to include everyone in the United States and Canada with the last name of Mitchell. They were arranged in geographical order beginning at Alameda, California, and expanding outward across the rest of the country. Griff hoped to eventually find either Gordon Mitchell himself or one of his descendants.

Griff knew that a few paragraphs and a couple of photos in the newspaper would not be enough to convince Dorian that he had been wrong all these years. A dragon could be stubborn to the point of arrogance, and Dorian was every inch a dragon. But if Griff could give him proof he could hold in his claws, Dorian might just return to the skies where he belonged.

So far, Griff was not sure what form that proof might take. On Sunday, he had called every Mitchell in the Alameda area, and none of them were related to airmail pilot Gordon Mitchell—though a few wanted to know if Griff would be signing books again soon. (Since the paperback rights had already been purchased, he assured them that another book tour was in the works.)

When he arrived back at the cave, he found the local telephone directory sitting on top of the listings Bear had printed. A yellow sticky note was stuck to the cover.

"It's a long shot, but your search might be over!" read the note in Bear's handwriting.

Another sticky note protruded from between the pages. Griff opened the phone book to the flagged page. A single stripe of fluorescent yellow ink highlighted the listing "MITCHELL, G W, III." The address was mere minutes away in nearby Fort Collins. Griff hit the button on the speakerphone and dialed the number.

"Hello?" said a woman's voice.

"I'm sorry to bother you," said Griff. "My name is Errington Felzworth Griffin. May I speak to Mr. Mitchell?"

"My husband's at work right now. Did you say you were Errington Felzworth Griffin?"

"Yes, I did."

"Oh, my goodness! You live over in Collinsfort Village, don't you?"

"Yes, I do."

"Gordon and I love your book! We were out of town when you signed copies at the Fort Collins Galleria!"

"Perhaps I could take care of that if you'd be willing to help me."

"In what way?"

"I'm doing some research for a magazine article about the early days of the airmail service, and I'm looking for information on an airmail pilot named Gordon Mitchell. He flew the Honolulu-to-San Francisco route in the 1930s."

"Yes! We *can* help you! Gordon Mitchell was my husband's grandfather!"

"*Good job, Bear!*" thought Griff.

"May I call back this evening when your husband's available?" he asked.

"I don't think he'd mind if you called him at work right now. He's a broadcast engineer at the time station."

"WWV? The station that broadcasts the time from the atomic clock in Boulder?"

"Yes. Would you like the number?"

"Yes, please!"

He jotted down the number and thanked her. But before dialing, he paused and took a few deep breaths while waiting for his racing heart to slow to a normal beat. "Easy, Griff. Be professional. You're a historian now, not a novelist. You don't want him to clam up on you."

He dialed the phone number Mrs. Mitchell had given him. The phone rang twice at the other end.

"WWV, this is Gordon."

"Mr. Mitchell?"

"Yes, who's calling?"

"Mr. Mitchell, my name is Errington Felzworth Griffin. Your wife gave me this number. If you have a few moments, I'd like to ask you some questions about your grandfather Gordon Mitchell. I'm writing a magazine article about early airmail pilots."

"Who did you say you were?"

"Errington Griffin. I'm an author."

"Oh, you wrote that chess book!"

"Yes, the same. I'd be happy to autograph your copy, even if you're unable to help me with my research."

"I'll do what I can! What would you like to know?"

"Your wife spoke of your grandfather in the past-tense. Shall I presume he's no longer with us?"

"That's right. He passed away about five years ago. He was eighty-seven."

Griff was relieved to hear that the near-collision had not affected Mitchell's longevity.

"Did he talk much about his days in the airmail service?"

"Oh, Lordy, only all the time! Once you got him started, he could go on all night!"

"Did he ever say anything about an item that appeared in the newspapers on July 3, 1937?"

"I don't know. What was it about?"

"The article said he nearly collided with something very large over the Pacific while flying the mail from Honolulu to San Francisco during a storm."

Gordon paused before answering. "He, uh, mentioned it from time to time."

Griff asked his next question in a calm tone, hoping not to sound intimidating. "Did he ever tell you what he nearly collided with?"

Once more, Gordon seemed to be considering his reply. "No, he never told anyone else—I mean, he never told anyone."

Griff's eyebrows rose a bit. "Mr. Mitchell, I have one more question, and I'll fully understand if you hang up on me without answering it. If you do, I promise I won't call you back."

Gordon took a deep breath and exhaled. "Go ahead."

"Mr. Mitchell, did your grandfather's plane nearly collide with a dragon?"

After a momentary pause, Gordon shot back his reply in staccato bursts. "Tomorrow's my day off. I'll be home all day. Come by any time. My address is in the phone book. We'll talk more then."

The line fell silent.

CHAPTER 15

Tangible Evidence

It was well past sundown, and the stars were flickering to life in the night sky when Griff landed at the edge of the cliff. At the same time, Bear brought his Suburban to a halt outside the cave, hopped from the driver's seat and closed the vehicle's door.

"Thanks again for dinner at Di Pasquale's, Griff. And it *isn't* even my birthday!"

"Well, you earned it, Bear. That was some remarkable detective work."

"Heck, if that's your price for opening a phone book, just ask me anytime." Bear headed to the cave. "Now, if you'll excuse me, I've got to catch the Overnight Express, Morpheus—the god of sleep—is calling, and it is a school night, you know."

Griff spent a few minutes gazing out at the lights of Collinsfort Village. He could see Dorian's rented hangar, but he couldn't tell if the lights were on.

"I have a feeling it will all be over soon, dear friend," he said softly through the night air. "Someone like you shouldn't be crying himself to sleep every night."

Griff went inside. Bear had already gone to bed, but Griff sat down at his writing desk. When he could not sleep, Griff wrote. And tonight, he knew he would not be getting much sleep.

He switched on the lamp and his Selectric, and rolled a clean sheet of paper into the machine. After typing his name, address and phone number in the upper left corner, he advanced the paper to the center of the page and typed a title and byline.

```
The Dragon and the Airmail Pilot:
   A True-Life Detective Story
   by Errington Felzworth Griffin
```

Griff drafted about eight pages of his and Dorian's history before a severe case of Noddinghead's Syndrome set in. He yawned, switched off the lamp and the typewriter, and called it a night.

The next morning, after a quick breakfast (a half-box of Cocoa Grenades, a quart of milk and eight slices of toast with black raspberry preserves), Griff flew to the city limits of Fort Collins. As he walked the rest of the way, he wondered if it was a good omen that Gordon Mitchell III lived in a house on Griffin Place. Griff dropped to all fours to reach the doorbell under the front porch awning.

Gordon opened the door. He was in his late thirties, with wire rim glasses and hair just beginning to turn gray. Realizing that Griff was much too tall to come inside, Gordon said, "Oh, um… back yard."

"I'll meet you there," said Griff. He stepped around the corner and over the fence.

Gordon slid open the patio door and joined Griff outside. He was carrying a copy of Griff's book and what appeared to be a photo album.

"First things first," said Griff as he sat down on the grass. He took a pen from his wallet while Gordon held the book toward him. "And who is this to?"

"Gordon and Heather."

Griff signed the book and handed it back. He spotted a copy of *The Mayflower Griffin* lying on the patio table.

"I see you're also a fan of Karolyne von Frankenburgh!" said Griff, fighting the urge to autograph that book as well.

Gordon picked up *The Mayflower Griffin*. "This? It belongs to my son. You know, kids his age can't get enough of this junk."

Griff deflated like a hot air balloon that had split a seam, but he tried to maintain his composure. "I… I understand it's quite an enjoyable story," he said, hoping not to sound defensive.

A look of bewilderment crossed Gordon's face as he recalled Griff's appearance on *The Tonight Show.*

Griff quickly changed his delivery. "Well, so I've been told. Enjoyable, perhaps—but junk, nonetheless."

Gordon silently read the book's synopsis from the slipcover. "Look, no offense intended," he said, "but I'll believe a griffin helped the *Mayflower* get here in one piece when I see a pig fly." He tossed the book aside. "Now, what would you like to know about my grandfather?"

Before Griff could answer, he was interrupted by the maniacal bark of a rottweiler in the adjacent back yard. Griff rolled his eyes in the dog's direction and then looked back at Gordon.

"Excuse me," he said. He leaned over the fence, opened his sharp beak and plunged his enormous head into the adjoining yard. He slammed his beak shut with a loud CRACK! and the rottweiler yelped once. Then there was silence.

Griff straightened up to find Gordon staring at him in ashen-faced disbelief.

"You… you didn't," Gordon stammered. "Did you?"

"Of course not. I only reminded him that it's not polite

125

to bark at people who are minding their own business in their own back yard."

Through the fence slats, Gordon could see the dog pacing nervously, but quietly.

Griff opened his wallet to its built-in spiral-bound notebook. "Mr. Mitchell, you ended our phone conversation rather abruptly."

"Well, it didn't take ears the size of yours to tell that I had let the cat out of the bag. Yes, it *was* a dragon. Granddad never told anyone until after he had retired. He didn't want to be grounded."

"Would he have been declared unfit to fly if he said he saw a dragon?"

"No, it wasn't that. It was because he saw one so far from home. Everyone knew that the nearest dragon lived in Santa Barbara. Granddad was more worried about being accused of drifting off course."

"Actually, the dragon is the one who was off course. He told me so himself."

"Is that the same dragon who's painting the mural in Collinsfort Village? I read something about it in the paper."

"Quite possibly."

"How do you know it was him? Did *he* ever tell anyone about it?"

"Only recently. To this day, he believes it was Amelia Earhart's plane. He thinks he's the reason she never completed her flight around the world, and he hasn't flown since."

"Wow." Gordon stared into space and thought over what he had just heard. "Talk about one long guilt trip," he mused. "So, what's this article of yours going to be about?"

"The working title is 'The Dragon and the Airmail Pilot,'

though if you prefer, I'll swap the billing and mention your grandfather first."

"No, that's fine. I'm sure Granddad wouldn't mind."

"If all goes well, it will be both a history of your grandfather's career in the airmail service and the story of Dorian—that's the dragon's name—returning to the air. I need some proof that it wasn't Amelia Earhart's plane he encountered."

Gordon slid the album across the patio table. "Everything you need is right here. This is Granddad's scrapbook."

Griff put on his reading glasses and picked up the scrapbook. He leafed through newspaper clippings, pages from flight logs, commendations, awards and numerous photos, including a few full-length shots of Gordon Mitchell's plane.

"This is perfect!"

"Turn a couple more pages. You'll find something particularly interesting."

The next few pages held clippings of the 1937 newspaper articles Griff had seen at the library. Opposite the clippings was a small medal depicting Saint George slaying a dragon.

"I didn't know you were Catholic," said Griff.

"I'm not. And neither was Granddad. Still, he never flew without that medal. You can take it out before you show the book to your friend, if you want."

"He's a big boy," replied Griff. "I'm sure he'll find it amusing."

CHAPTER 16

Book of Revelation

Around two in the afternoon, Dorian called it a day and strolled into the forest for an early dinner. He noticed that his vest was fitting more snugly than usual, so he caught only one moose. He consumed every bit of the moose, including its antlers, bones and hide. (A dragon really can eat almost anything; though, even dragons must be especially careful of fish bones.)

After dinner, he ambled out of the woods. As he reached the road back to town, he froze in his tracks. "What are you doing here?" he asked warily.

Next to a large sign that said, "WILDERNESS PERMITS ONLY BEYOND THIS POINT" sat Griff, cradling the scrapbook in his lap. "Sit down, Dorian. It's story time," he said.

"But it's only Tuesday."

"This story can't wait until Saturday," said Griff.

As Dorian sat down—now more curious than suspicious—Griff opened the scrapbook and pretended he was reading from it. "Once upon a time, there was a dragon named Dorian. He was as blue as a peacock with eyes the color of jade. And Dorian loved to fly. One day in the summer of 1937, Dorian flew right into aviation history. Or so he thought…."

Dennis stepped out from behind the sign. He was wearing a corduroy beret, a rumpled sweater, knickers and old shoes with a pair of knee-high socks. His left arm held a stack of newspapers. "Get your San Francisco *Bay Herald!*" he cried, holding up a reprint of a newspaper from 1937. "First edition! Latest news! Amelia Earhart's plane disappears over the Pacific! Read it right here! Morning paper! Get your *Bay Herald*!"

A man emerged from the same hiding place. He was dressed in a pinstripe suit and a hat. "Say, son, I'll take one of those," he said.

"That'll be a nickel!"

The man flipped a coin into the air and Dennis caught it. "Thanks, mister!" He handed the man a newspaper. "Ain't it awful about that lady pilot?"

"Sure is, son. Just terrible." The man opened the paper and did a slapstick double take. "Say, take a gander at this!" He held the paper in front of Dennis.

"Sorry, mister, I never learned how to read. The newspaper man tells me what's on the front page so I'll know what to yell to sell my papers."

"Well, it says here that Gordon Mitchell landed his plane at the airport here in San Francisco, and they had to help him out of the cockpit. I know Gordon. He's an airmail pilot on the San Francisco-to-Honolulu run, and a darned good one, too!"

"Why'd they have to help him? Was he drunk, mister? Did he pass out?"

"No, no, nothing like that! Seems he was jabbering about nearly colliding with something over the Pacific."

"Wow! You mean he almost crashed into another plane?"

"Not quite. Says here that whatever it was, it didn't make any engine noise, and it was a heck of a lot bigger than any airplane. I wonder what it could have been."

"Yeah, me too!" said Dennis. "What's bigger than an airplane and doesn't make any noise when it flies?"

They both stroked their chins while thinking.

"I've got it!" declared Dennis. "It was a blimp with its engines turned off! I'll bet there were Nazi spies inside!"

The man pored over the newspaper again. "Hmm... couldn't be a blimp; Gordon said it climbed out of the clouds and then dived right back in."

"Yeah, I guess a blimp couldn't do that."

After a few more moments of chin stroking, the man snapped his fingers. "Son, have you ever heard of Dorian di Drago?"

"No, mister. We have a radio at home, but my dad doesn't like opera."

"No, no, son. He's not an opera singer. He's an artist—a dragon who paints murals. Lives down in Santa Barbara, about three hundred miles or so from here. They say he's as tall as a four story building, and that's a lot bigger than an airplane."

"Yeah! And a dragon doesn't have engines, so he wouldn't make any noise when he flies! But what's he doing three hundred miles from home?"

"Well, yesterday there was an awful nasty storm out over the Pacific. It could have blown him hundreds of miles out of his way. You know, the weather *has* done stranger things—like the day it rained frogs over the Midwest."

"Frogs?"

"Yessiree! A tornado sucked all the frogs out of a pond, and when it petered out, the frogs came raining down from the sky."

"Wow! Raining frogs and dragons crashing into airplanes! Blame it on the weather, eh, mister?"

"Yeah, son! Blame it on the weather!"

Griff began applauding. "Bravo! Bravo! Let's hear it for the Collinsfort Village Players!"

Dorian, looking a bit irritated, joined the applause.

Griff continued. "Our Newsboy was played by Dennis Pearson."

Dennis stepped forward and took a bow.

"And the Man on the Street was played by our special guest from Fort Collins, Gordon Mitchell III, grandson of airmail pilot Gordon Mitchell," said Griff.

Gordon bowed and approached Dorian. He held out his right hand.

"Uh, pleased to meet you—I think," said Dorian as he leaned forward to shake Gordon's hand. Dorian appeared utterly bewildered. "Have we been introduced?"

"No, but you *did* come pretty close to meeting Granddad in person," said Gordon.

"Right," said Dorian, still confused. "Um, how close?"

"Well, we could say you might have been picking pieces of propeller out of your teeth if Granddad hadn't pulled back on the stick and opened the throttle all the way."

"Ah, of course!" said Dorian with an exaggerated nod and a big grin. "Would you excuse me for a moment?"

He stood up and stepped over to where Griff was sitting. Crouching down, he wrapped his wings halfway around himself and Griff for a little privacy. He spoke barely above a whisper.

"Is there anyone on this side of the Rockies who you haven't told about me and Amelia Earhart? And I don't know where you found this guy, but he's giving me an industrial-strength case of the heebie-jeebies. I did some homework, Griff. Amelia Earhart was flying that plane and Fred Noonan was her navigator, not some joker named Gordon Mitchell. There wasn't another soul in the air for hundreds of miles around, so how did this phony-baloney find out about me nearly crashing into her plane? You don't suppose someone who looks like a griffin and smells like a rat told him, do you?"

Griff held up the scrapbook. "Dorian, it wasn't Amelia Earhart's plane, and I can prove it."

"With pictures of your graduation from Stool Pigeon University?" Dorian took his reading glasses from his vest pocket.

"This is Gordon Mitchell *the First's* scrapbook," said Griff.

Dorian took the scrapbook and gave the first few pages a quick glance. When he arrived at the full-length photograph of Gordon Mitchell and his plane, his face drained of all expression. But as he studied the picture, he began to light up as the revelation slowly dawned on him.

"It's true!" he whispered with a broad smile. "It wasn't Amelia Earhart! *This* is the plane! I'd recognize it anywhere!"

He turned a few more pages and read the newspaper accounts of the near-collision. As Griff had expected, Dorian chuckled when he saw the Saint George medal.

"You have no reason to stay on the ground anymore," Griff said. "The skies are all yours again."

Dorian beamed like a gambler watching three JACKPOT symbols land on the pay line of a slot machine, but the smile soon melted into a worried look. "What about *him*?" he said, tipping his head in Gordon's direction. "I mean, what am I supposed to say? 'Nice weather we're having. Oh, and yes, I'm the winged monstrosity that ended your grandfather's illustrious career.'"

"Keep reading."

Dorian turned past the medal and saw the awards and commendations that had been bestowed on Gordon Mitchell. The last item in the scrapbook was Mitchell's obituary. The rest of the pages were empty. "Eighty-seven. Very impressive. I thought I might have at least scared him out of a few years' growth."

Dorian stood up and walked back over to Gordon. "*So* pleased to meet you!" he said, dropping to his knees and thrusting his right claw forward. He shook hands so vigorously that he nearly lifted Gordon off the ground.

Then, grinning broadly in appreciation, he held out the scrapbook, which Gordon—after flexing his arm to restore its proper movement—accepted.

Dorian took a couple of steps back and stood with his wings folded and his arms at his sides. He looked into the sky for a few moments before drawing a deep breath and squatting down into takeoff position. "Guys," he said, still gazing into the wild blue yonder, "if this doesn't work, make sure they bury me in Santa Barbara."

"Get on with it!" barked Griff.

"Gentlemen! May I have a countdown, please?"

Griff, Dennis and Gordon counted together. "Five… four… three…"

Dorian's scales shimmered in the late afternoon sun as he quivered with anticipation.

"…two… ONE!"

"LIFTOFF!" roared Dorian.

A cobalt blue rocket shot into the sky above the Rocky Mountains. A moment before gravity kicked in, Dorian extended his colossal wings, and after a few awkward initial flaps and flutters, he was soon arching gracefully across the skies. The ground below was inundated in a swirling sea of colors projected by the membranes in Dorian's wings.

Griff joined Dorian in the air.

"It's like riding a bike!" cried Dorian, turning a perfect loop-the-loop. "You never forget how!"

"But you've never ridden a bike," said Griff.

"Oh, yeah." Dorian plummeted like a stone while clawing at the air and emitting cartoonish shrieks of terror. Less than a hundred feet from the ground, he pulled out of the dive and returned to where Griff was circling.

"Welcome back," said Griff. "It's been pretty dull up here without you, old friend." As if on cue, a small convocation of bald eagles joined the winged giants.

"Hi, guys!" Dorian bellowed. "Did you miss your old pal Dorian?" He held out a single claw and an eagle alighted on it. The eagle rolled his head from side to side, scrutinizing the airborne blue Colossus. Satisfied that Dorian wasn't some monstrous aberration, the eagle flitted away.

Griff and Dorian returned to the ground.

"Is that pocket on the back of your vest what I think it is?" asked Griff.

"It *is*!" said Dorian. He had not used one of the vest's special features in decades. He took the vest off, spread it out on the ground and opened a large pocket located between the wing slits. From it he unrolled a rope ladder and assembled a harness that was just the right size for securing one or two human-sized passengers. He put the vest back on and dropped to his claws and knees.

"You must be in good physical health and free of back problems, heart disorders or motion sickness to ride this attraction," said Dorian in a very official voice. "Upon boarding, please sit all the way back in the seat and fasten the safety restraints."

"You mean us?" said Gordon in momentary shock.

"I don't see anyone else who'd fit in there," replied Dorian.

Gordon and Dennis scrambled up the rope ladder as if they were the first passengers on a brand-new roller coaster. While they strapped themselves in, Griff cupped his claws in front of his beak and mimicked the nasal tones of a loudspeaker.

"For your safety, please remain seated with your hands and arms inside the ride at all times." Then Griff wrapped his talons around an imaginary floor-mounted brake lever. When Dennis and Gordon were securely buckled in, Griff pulled the invisible lever and mimicked the "Whoosh!" of a released air brake.

Dorian gently reared up to a forty-five-degree angle and looked over his shoulder. "Hang on tight. Take-off is always the roughest part of the ride."

"How rough?" asked Gordon raising an eyebrow.

"Like an aircraft carrier's catapult, only straight up."

Dennis grinned broadly. "Let's do it!"

Dorian faced forward and assumed launch position once more.

From where they sat, Dennis and Gordon saw nothing but sky beyond Dorian's massive head. A split second later, the rushing wind had plastered them back in their seats and was trying to make Gordon's glasses into a permanent part of his face.

"Holy flippin' moly!" Gordon yelled over the rushing wind.

"Whoa, awesome!" Dennis shouted.

Dorian leveled off and slowed to a calm glide, barely flapping his wings. "How are you two doing back there?"

"Great!" yelled Dennis, taking in the panoramic view of the Rockies. "I can see my house from here! And there's the library!"

"What else have you got?" asked Gordon grinning from ear to ear.

"Well, I missed the jet age. All I know are some old barnstorming stunts," said Dorian.

"Bring it on!" Gordon whooped.

Dorian arched over into a death spiral and buzzed a herd of deer into a mad dash for cover. After a series of barrel rolls, he climbed straight up and disappeared above the clouds. From his high vantage point Dorian located a clearing on a perpetually snow-covered peak and landed on all fours. He scooped up a huge claw full of snow and shaped it into a sphere the size of a large beach ball. "It's been ages since I nailed ol' Erry with one of these!"

"And it'll be even longer if ol' Dory gets nailed first," said a voice from behind them. There stood Griff, repeatedly tossing and catching an equally large snowball.

"No fair!" cried Dorian. "I'm carrying passengers!"

"Then I suppose we need to choose up sides," said Griff.

"Okay, you and me against them."

"I was thinking of something more balanced," said Griff in a parental tone, "like Gordon and I against Dennis and you... big person, smaller critter versus little person, bigger critter."

"But I want Gordon on my side!" said Dorian while Dennis and Gordon descended the rope ladder to the ground. "Look at those arms! The guy obviously works out!"

"Dorian, it's all academic. You're going to lose anyway because you're the biggest target," explained Griff as he stowed the ladder inside Dorian's vest pocket.

Dorian stood up. "Which is why you won't mind if I do... THIS!" He pasted Griff squarely in the face with the snowball then scooped up more snow and leaped into the air, shaping his next snowball as he climbed.

"For that you *shall* pay dearly, dragon!" Griff roared. He returned fire while taking to the air after Dorian.

What should have been a genteel team competition erupted into a free-for-all of snowballs flying in every direction over the clearing. The commotion drew the attention of a timber wolf that stood at the edge of the clearing and looked on curiously.

As Griff had predicted, Dorian became everyone's favorite victim. Pummeled from both the air and the ground, he dropped his snowball, clutched his chest in mock agony and (despite being a bachelor) wailed, "Tell my wife I love her!" He feigned a crash landing and slid to a halt just a few feet from the wolf. He raised his head momentarily to stare at the comparatively mouse-sized, very puzzled animal. Then he scrambled to his feet calling, "Run for your lives! It's the Big Bad Wolf!"

He raced to the other side of the clearing and dropped to the ground while Griff landed and quickly unrolled the rope ladder. Dennis and Gordon scampered into Dorian's rumble seat, and the foursome beat a hasty retreat the likes of which Groucho, Chico, Harpo and Zeppo would have envied.

CHAPTER 17

A Double Treat

Granny and the Big Bad Wolf sat side by side on the library's atrium steps, listening to Griff read from a large, leather and gold bound storybook. On the step below sat Little Red Riding Hood and Chris. Toad, Mole, Rat and a few more of the Collinsfort Village children were sitting nearby while Badger claimed a comfy overstuffed chair. Goldilocks and the Three Bears shared a picnic lunch with Kyle and Cindy, and the Fox perched the Gingerbread Man on his head for a better view. Outside the story circle, over by the window, Dennis was plopped into a beanbag chair with his nose buried in a copy of Karolyne von Frankenburgh's *Prince of the Sky.*

Dorian lowered his massive body to the ground and stretched out on his side. He propped himself up on his left elbow and studied the life-size likenesses of Granny and the Big Bad Wolf. "I'll need some number three cyan on a palette and a detail brush, Dennis," he said.

Dennis meandered among the gallon paint cans until he found the one labeled NO 3 CYAN. He dipped one of Dorian's brushes into the can and drew a small spot of paint on a palette the size of a party tray.

"Thank you," said Dorian as Dennis set the palette in his left claw. Concentrating all of his muscle control into the tips of his fingers, Dorian daubed the smallest drop of paint into the irises of the Big Bad Wolf's eyes to add some sparkling highlights. "That should just about do it," he said, examining the effect.

He handed Dennis the palette and hoisted himself up just enough to slither over to the lower right corner of the mural. "Time for the finishing touch. We'll need a four-inch brush, another detail brush, and the number eight yellow and number six indigo in the cans."

"Number eight yellow and number six indigo," Dennis repeated. "Got it!" With the brushes tucked under his arm, he waded once more into the sea of paint cans and returned with a can in each hand.

"And this," said Dorian, "is what makes it a genuine 'di Drago.'" He dipped the broad paintbrush in the yellow paint and laid down a thick eight-inch by sixteen-inch rectangle of paint exactly two feet in from the mural's corner. Bearing down slightly with the detail brush, Dorian drew an indigo frame within the yellow rectangle. Then, in a series of quick strokes, he created his distinctive DdiD monogram. "It is now officially a di Drago mural," he announced as he rose to his knees.

He reached into one of his trunks and hauled out an orange electrical extension cord. "I think there's an outlet just inside the service door," he said, handing Dennis the end with the plug. Dennis ran around to the back of the library while Dorian attached an industrial hot air gun to the extension cord. By the time Dennis came back, Dorian had stretched out on his side again, switched on the hot air gun and was sweeping it back and forth across the freshly painted monogram.

Dennis began laughing.

"Yeah, yeah, I know," said Dorian. "What's wrong with *this* picture?"

"I'm sorry," said Dennis. "I was expecting you to breathe some fire."

"Only a very small percentage of dragons can do that. Isn't it amazing how *they* get all the glory?"

A few minutes later, Dorian turned off the hot air gun and waited for the paint to cool. He ran a scaly finger over the monogram. "Feel that," he said.

Dennis stroked the surface of the monogram and smiled when he felt how the deep blue frame and lettering had sunk into the yellow background. "That's neat!"

Dorian stood up and began coiling the extension cord while Dennis went to unplug it. "Madame Mayor, it's all yours!" he called to Justine.

Mayor Pearson sat next to a camera tripod at the top of a wheeled platform about half the height of the mural. She stood up and opened the 50-millimeter lens on her digital camera. While Dorian and Dennis collected the paint cans and other paraphernalia, she composed a tightly cropped photo through the camera's viewer. She took one shot, checked it on the camera's display and then took several more for backup. After packing up the camera and tripod, Justine descended to the ground and released the brakes on the platform's wheels. With help from her husband Andrew, she began to push it away from the library.

"Let me help you with that," said Dorian.

"Stay!" ordered Mayor Pearson. "I want to take a few shots of you by the mural."

"Better do what she says," quipped Andrew. "After all, she's the boss!"

An hour later, Justine had captured Dorian in a dozen photos. The compositions ranged from a smiling Dorian leaning casually against the library, to an imposing low-angle shot of the towering dragon spreading his mighty wings and peering down over his crossed, muscular arms with a studious scowl. A photo lab in Fort Collins would soon be churning out hundreds of eight by ten enlargements to be handed out as souvenirs at the unveiling.

Inside the library, another exhibition was being readied. Dennis' sketches had chronicled the mural's creation so perfectly that the Arts Council had them professionally matted and framed. The exhibition was called "The Library Mural: The Work in Progress." Art critics from Fort Collins and Denver who attended a preview were amazed when they were told the artist was a mere eleven years old.

Justine and Andrew dismantled the platform and stowed the parts in their Chevy Blazer.

"Come on, Dennis!" said Andrew. "It's time to go!"

Dennis climbed into the back seat of the Blazer, and the First Family of Collinsfort Village headed home.

Dorian sorted through the contents of his trunks and pulled out a folded white tarpaulin marked 50'X50'. He set the tarp on the roof, unfurled it and allowed it to drape all the way to the ground, covering the mural. Using a length of gold satin rope long enough to encircle the building, Dorian secured the tarp with a slipknot and coiled up the rest of the rope on the roof.

After putting away his trunks, he set off on foot for the woods to have dinner. He could have flown, but he wanted to give the people of Collinsfort Village an extra surprise at the unveiling.

Three days later, the library's courtyard resembled a storybook characters convention, with citizens and city officials mingling in costume under sunny skies. Bear, in full Franciscan monk's regalia, was the Minor Canon to Griff's Griffin. The seven members of the Collinsfort Village city council were the Seven Dwarfs, allthough Justine "Snow White" Pearson and her Prince Charming were nowhere to be seen. Neither was Dorian.

Dennis chose to deviate from the storybook theme and dressed up as Michelangelo, capturing the day's events in his sketch pad, which he had set up on an easel. His older brother sweltered in an elaborate dragon costume. Even Gordon Mitchell III and his family traveled from Fort Collins to attend the unveiling. Gordon's son was dressed as (what else?) a griffin wearing a black Pilgrim's hat.

At eleven o'clock sharp, Griff strode to the front of the throng and stood before the veiled library wall. He faced the crowd and opened a giant prop storybook.

"Once upon a time," he said, "there was a dragon named Dorian. He was as blue as a peacock, with eyes the color of jade. He could paint a mural as beautifully as any of the masters. And when Dorian flew, his wings turned the skies above and the earth below into rainbows."

Suddenly the courtyard was swept into a whirlpool of colors. Shrieks of surprise and a tidal wave of applause surged from the crowd as Dorian, his wings beating the air and blazing with colors, circled overhead. The magnificent dragon landed gently on all fours.

"What, you've never seen a dragon fly?" said Dorian with a wily grin at the crowd. The audience laughed, cheered, and then applauded as he folded his wings, revealing Snow White and Prince Charming in his vest's rumble seat.

Andrew Pearson unrolled the rope ladder, and he and Justine climbed down to the ground.

Mayor Pearson held her scepter (a camouflaged wireless microphone) to her lips. "Good townsfolk, hear me! By the power vested in me as Princess of Storybook Land and Mayor of Collinsfort Village, I declare this day 'Dorian di Drago Day.'"

Dorian stood up and took a deep bow as he basked in the applause.

Justine continued when the noise had settled down.

"Be it known from here to the ends of the earth, that the esteemed artist vows to return to our fair village every year on or about this date in order to maintain and preserve his work of art. It is, therefore, my civic and royal duty to introduce to you, Dorian di Drago—muralist extraordinaire—upon whom I confer the privilege of unveiling his creation for all to see."

"My pleasure, Mayor Princess," said Dorian. "But before the veil comes off, I'd like to thank all of you for your hospitality and for letting me use your library as a canvas. I know that when I come back to touch up the mural I'll feel right at home all over again.

"I also want to thank Gordon Mitchell III who dropped by from Fort Collins. All this time, he never knew that he possessed the truth about why I gave up flying nearly a century ago. The truth came out when Griff, Dennis and Bear teamed up to find it, and because of them, I'm back in the air where I belong. Griff's story of the event will be in tomorrow's edition of the Collinsfort Village *Chronicle*. Guys, I can't thank you enough."

Dorian turned to his friends and led the applause as they took a bow.

"And now, for the reason we're all here today," Dorian continued. "Two of you are going to help me unveil the mural. If you were here early enough to get a souvenir photo before we ran out, please take the picture out of its protective cover and read what it says on the back."

Evelyn the librarian, who was dressed as Cinderella, began screaming while Carl Lumbly, in Daniel Boone attire, shouted, "All right!" and waved his photo in the air. Both were holding a picture that bore Dorian's handwritten message, "On the wings of a dragon you shall fly this very day." They made their way to the front of the crowd.

Evelyn and Carl strapped themselves in, and Dorian dangled the end of the satin rope in front of them. "Hold on tight," he said. "We don't want to lose either of you." They tightened their grip on both the rope and the harness straps. Dorian took hold of the rope, too, so the strain would not yank Evelyn and Carl's arms from their sockets. He grinned once more at the crowd and hunkered down for takeoff.

"Ladies and gentlemen! Boys and girls! I now present *Story Time at the Library with Griff*!" Dorian rocketed into the sky. The rope tightened, pulling apart the slipknot and dropping the veil. Though many in the crowd had followed the mural's progress from its first faint outlines, seeing the finished masterpiece for the first time was truly exciting. The cheering and applauding went on until well after Dorian and his passengers had landed.

With the day's festivities complete, it was time for Dorian to fly home to Santa Barbara. It had been decades since he made such a long trip by air, and he was afraid he might lose his way, so Griff agreed to join him. Griff only needed to correct Dorian's course twice during the two-day trip, and neither deviation was serious.

"It's a pity we won't get to see the Strip at night," Dorian lamented the next morning as they swooped over the opulent resort hotels of Las Vegas in the already broiling sun.

"Dorian, you can come back and see it any time you want," said Griff.

Dorian chuckled. "You're right! I keep forgetting that I'm not tied to the ground anymore."

When they landed at the seaside airport in Santa Barbara, they hardly drew a second glance. At home, Dorian was an artist first and a dragon second. To his fellow Santa Barbara residents, his flying ability came in a distant third. An airport groundskeeper brought his maintenance cart to a halt and remarked, "Hey, was that you doing that, you know—all those colors in the sky and on the ground?" He illustrated by twirling a finger overhead.

"Yep, that was me, Lou!" said Dorian. He keyed in the security code that opened the hangar doors.

"Huh! I never even *knew* you could fly," said Lou, no more amazed than if Dorian had been wearing a new vest. He stepped on the gas pedal and the cart puttered away.

For a moment Griff was confused by the seemingly cool reaction, but he quickly caught on. "Welcome to California," he muttered as he followed Dorian into the hangar.

"You've got it, pal," said Dorian.

When Dorian had finished unpacking, he and Griff headed for Dorian's fishing island, guided by the dragon's recuperated navigational senses.

About two hours after leaving the coast of Santa Barbara Griff asked, "Is that it?" His sharp eagle eyes had spotted a tiny green dot of land on the horizon well before Dorian could discern it. Dorian was still navigating astronomically.

"It's got to be. The next island is at least two hundred miles farther."

Dorian smiled as the land mass loomed closer. "Yep, that's the place!"

The two friends landed and strolled along the sandy beach. Gentle sea ripples lapped at the shore while lofty palm trees swayed lazily under the trade winds.

"It's as beautiful as I remember!" said Dorian in an almost prayer-like voice.

At one end of the island, a herd of sea lions basked under the afternoon sun.

"Ah, they're still stopping here on the way to Chile!" said Dorian.

Griff raised a claw and stopped short, gesturing for Dorian to do the same. "We're going to scare them away," he whispered.

"Are you nuts? They *love* me! They're probably wondering where ol' Dorian has been all these years. I'll introduce you to them, and we'll all go for a swim together!"

But as they drew nearer, pandemonium broke out. Within seconds every last sea lion had fled the island in a mad, noisy rush to the sea. Dorian and Griff stood side by side on the deserted beach and watched the entire herd head out to open waters.

Dorian sighed. "It'll probably take fifty years for them to get used to me again."

The two friends continued their walk until they had circled the island and caught up to their own footprints in the sand.

Dorian began unbuttoning his vest. "Well, let's eat," he said.

"Keep your vest on!" Griff barked. "Dinner's on *me* this time." He slipped his wallet off over his head, unzipped it and took out a watertight license holder. "Did you know that out-of-state visitors can apply for one of these over the phone?" he said, holding up his Special Non-Resident California Fish and Game License. He strapped the license around his upper left arm and lobbed his wallet in Dorian's direction. "Here, keep this dry for me!"

Dorian snagged the wallet by its lanyard and sat down in the sand.

Griff prowled the waters from an altitude of about a quarter-mile. Spotting his prey, he instinctively sounded his hunting cry, an ear-splitting combination of an eagle's screech and a lion's roar. He rolled into a swift, steep dive, extended his claws and plowed into the sea with a cascading splash until only his wings were visible above the surface. In the tumble of foam and sea spray, Dorian caught the flash of a large, grayish-white tail fin. A moment later, Griff raised his head out of the water with a smile of satisfaction. He began flapping his wings forcefully.

Dorian stared in wonder as Griff hoisted an enormous great white shark into the air. The shark was easily ten feet longer than Griff's height.

"It doesn't get any fresher than this!" Griff roared. He broke into a laugh that chilled Dorian's marrow, for the laugh was a remnant of the victory cry Griff would have uttered had he just defeated a dragon in battle. The dazed shark began to shake off the blow and tried to thrash its way out of Griff's crushing grasp. "So, Mr. 'JAWS,' you think you're a tough guy, do you?" said Griff. The shark flailed about with even more intensity. "Well, I'll teach YOU not to mess with MY friends on Amity Island, you overgrown anchovy!" He stopped the shark's thrashing with a single deep bite behind its gills, adding a menacing throaty growl for dramatic effect.

Dorian stood up and staggered to the water's edge, a bit shaken after watching Griff do to the shark what griffins had once done to dragons. He blinked himself back to the modern world and yelled, "You know, you've got enough there to feed *both* of us!"

"Exactly!" Griff shouted. He swung around toward the mainland.

"Hey, where are you going?" Dorian called after him. He leaped into the air and caught up to Griff in a few flaps of his wings. "We haven't eaten yet!"

"And we won't until we get back to Santa Barbara. This beauty is going to make the best rosemary-grilled shark steaks you ever tasted!"

Dorian reflected for a moment on Griff's battle cry and thought, *Yeah, grilled shark steak does sound good!*

CHAPTER 18

Epilogue

$\mathscr{A}$MELIA $\mathscr{E}$ARHART

DORIAN di DRAGO
Santa Barbara, California

Mixed Media — Gift of the Artist

Most photographs of Amelia Earhart portray her eyes fixed squarely on the camera. In this piece, however, I have chosen to interpret her gazing into the distance. She is looking toward Howland Island in the Pacific where a lighthouse now stands as a monument to her memory.

The pair of inlaid brickwork lines jutting from the base of the mural and extending across the Promenade toward the ocean may appear to be parallel. They are, in fact, converging ever so slightly. If extended, they would eventually intersect at the Earhart Light on Howland Island.

—DdiD

These words appeared on a small metal plaque below Dorian's most recent creation, as well as in the commemorative program that had been printed for the work's unveiling ceremony. An immense white tarpaulin shrouded both the mural and the plaque.

Dorian strode solemnly across the newly opened Earhart Promenade at the Museum of Aviation on the coast at Santa Monica, California. He took hold of a gold satin tassel and with a single tug dropped the veil, revealing the giant photo-realistic portrait and a huge bouquet of flowers lying at its base. The invited guests broke into passionate but dignified applause befitting the solemn occasion.

Dorian picked up the bouquet and cradled it tenderly in his arms. He turned toward the railing that enclosed the Promenade. As the last rays of the setting sun dipped below the Pacific horizon and could no longer cause his wings to throw off their flamboyant rainbows, Dorian launched himself into the twilight sky and set a course for Howland Island.

Bear laid two letters on Griff's writing table when he returned from shopping.

Griff picked up the one on top and stared at the Washington D.C. postmark. It was on an envelope he had addressed to himself on his own typewriter. The envelope weighed only enough to contain a single folded sheet of paper. With a sigh, he used a talon to neatly split the top of the envelope without disturbing the stamp. He unfolded the cream-colored linen bond letterhead and put on his reading glasses.

```
SMITHSONIAN MAGAZINE
Washington, DC


Mr. Errington Felzworth Griffin
P.O. Box 862
Collinsfort Village, CO  80524


Dear Mr. Griffin:


     After a thorough review of your submis-
sion, The Dragon and the Airmail Pilot: A
True-Life Detective Story, the editors of
Smithsonian magazine regret to inform you
that your work does not fit our editorial
needs.  As we do not anticipate our needs
changing in the near future, we wish you
every success in finding a suitable pub-
lication for your work.


Sincerely,
SMITHSONIAN MAGAZINE
Submissions Department
```

"I don't care what anyone says," commented Griff out loud to no one particular. "You *never* get used to seeing these things."

"What was that?" asked Bear as he put away the month's groceries.

"Oh, nothing."

Griff was about to wad up the letter and toss it into the

wastebasket when his eyes came to rest on the photograph Mayor Pearson had taken of Dorian in flight. Griff had mounted the photo in a montage frame along with newspaper clippings about the library mural, reproductions of Dennis' sketches, and pictures of both the elder and younger Gordon Mitchell.

"Can you do me a favor, Bear?"

"It depends. What do you need?"

Griff returned the letter to its envelope. "When you write up next month's shopping list, add an eight-and-a-half by eleven-inch certificate frame." He opened the second envelope—from Chrestus & Minos—and found a copy of a letter addressed to someone else in town.

```
(COURTESY COPY)

Mr. Dennis Pearson
28765 Rubens Circle
Collinsfort Village, CO  80524


Dear Mr. Pearson:


    Our art department has finished re-
viewing your portfolio. We have forwarded
it to Fräulein Karolyne von Frankenburgh
for her consideration. If she approves,
we will be one step closer to sending you
a contract.
    While waiting for her response, may
we request more samples of your work? We
would specifically like to see two or three
rough sketches of original art not based on
any existing illustrations or previously
```

```
published books.  To aid you in this, en-
closed please find a synopsis and selected
chapters from Fräulein von Frankenburgh's
most recent manuscript.  Pending a favor-
able review, a contract and a parental
consent form will be on their way.
    We look forward to seeing more of your
work.

Sincerely,
Maury Cendack
Art Director
```

"Make that two frames," said Griff. He looked out the window as a Chevy Blazer pulled up with Justine Pearson at the wheel. Dennis jumped from the vehicle and ran toward the front door, waving a letter over his head....

Born in Pennsylvania in 1955 and now living in Southern California, Joe Ekaitis is the middle child in a family of seven. His father William is a retired steelworker and his mother Frances retired from the founding staff of the library at California State University, San Bernardino. He acquired a strong work ethic from his father and a love of learning from his mother.

Joe discovered early in life that he enjoyed entertaining others. He entertained college students as the on-air personality "Jojo Scappezzi" at KVCR-FM, San Bernardino, California, and appeared as a six-foot singing raccoon on Chuck Barris' *The Gong Show.* Today, he maintains business communications systems for a Fortune 500 financial institution—but he hasn't lost his love for entertaining. He is currently the lead male soloist for the St. Mary's Catholic Church choir in Fontana, California, whose director is his wife, Cathy.

And Joe writes! With the publication of *Collinsfort Village*, he joins the ranks of American storytellers, a fellowship that includes such notables as L. Frank Baum, E. B. White, and Frank Stockton. He looks forward to the day when his writing and storytelling will stand beside theirs.